CW00859600

By the same author

Historical Fiction

Song of the Sea
The Shepherd of St Just
Where Seagulls Fly (2013 Edition)

Selected Other Fiction

The Black Rose
The Darkness Inside
Distance
Fey
For Love or Money
Heart's Desire
Into the Depths
The Liquid Room
Love & Other Oddities
Minos
Quiddity
Spontaneous Combustion
Sub-Zero
Synergy

Selected Non-Fiction

Enlightenment: One Man's Search for the Truth of Existence
Everyday Magic
Handbook for the Living Dead (under the name R.I.Peace)
Intuition: A User's Guide
Reality Perception: How such things as ESP & the Supernatural can exist
There is Only Now

Foreword

On the morning of Wednesday 25th March 2015 I woke with the song *The Hanging Tree* repeating itself incessantly in my mind. It is sung by the character of Katniss Everdeen in the movie *The Hunger Games: Mockingjay Part 1*, which I'd bought on DVD upon its release a couple of weeks before. Unusually for a new film, I'd only watched it twice and, at the point the song was discovered instilled in my brain, hadn't viewed it for quite a few days.

I have no idea why the song had such a strong presence in my mind upon waking and do not recall dreaming, but I could not shake it all morning, the lyrics repeating time and again. The tune evoked thoughts of the U.S. Deep South in the time of slavery and suggested particular atmospherics. I thought the title of the song would also be a good title for a book and simply began to write what came forth from my subconscious despite having had plans to write a very different, post-apocalyptic story. Within a week and a half, I had written this novella.

Many were the hours that I wrote with musical accompaniment. The play-list included the aforementioned *The Hanging Tree*, as well as *Freedom* by Anthony Hamilton feat. Elayna Boynton, *Ain't No Grave* by Johnny Cash, *All Washed Out* by Edward Sharpe & The Magnetic Zeroes, *Safe & Sound* by Taylor Swift feat. The Civil Wars and *Fire Escape* by Half Moon Run. In breaks from the writing these songs and others were often still playing and I also watched Tarantino's excellent *Django Unchained* a number of times.

The most influential of the songs mentioned above were the first two and it may be that playing them while reading this story, along with others of a similar ilk, could add to the emotion and atmosphere. I hope that what they have helped to inspire is a powerful tale that will resonate within you, having a deep and lasting effect.

This isn't a story about the politics of the time. Nor is it a story about the slave trade or American Civil War. It is the personal tale of two slaves whose love sustains them as they toil in the Louisiana heat.

Many people remain enslaved in a sense. They are slaves to their jobs and to money. More importantly, they are slaves to ideologies, conventions and dogma, just as the slave traders, owners and abusers were at the time when this story is set. Though these shackles are largely unseen, they are there nonetheless. Essentially, the human body may have freedom on the whole, but the human mind still awaits liberty. I hope that one day it will be attained and on that day we will truly become free.

iv

Prologue

She passed into the meadow. The cold light of dawn was diffused by a blanket of mist shrouding the wide river, bull rushes ghostly and still upon its near bank. Amidst the rough grasses stood the solitary willow, faint creaking issuing from its secretive shadows and creeping into the gathered hush. Tendrils of mist drifted above the bare earth at the foot of its wide trunk and a figure hung from one of the boughs above, gently swaying to and fro.

She approached through the paleness, a shadow in a dream. Her cheeks glistened, eyes filled with loss and speaking of a heart wrung tight by the sight revealed beneath the looming tree.

She fell to her knees, the grasses caressing her skin with the moisture of fading night. Her weeping was woven into the mist as she covered her face, bent and bowed by the weight of her grief.

Isaac sat at the shaded bench, face covered in a layer of perspiration as he held a piece of stale bread in one hand, the other cradling a dinted tin bowl. He lifted the bowl, taking a mouthful of the thin gruel within and following it with a bite of the bread.

Thoughtfully staring ahead as he chewed, Isaac looked beyond the end of the women's cabin and the bunkhouse. He watched as half a dozen farmhands gathered before the Big House, the sun glaring off its white walls and causing him to wince. They all carried guns, Silas at their centre with his pistol hug at his hip, barking orders from beneath the shadow of his wide-brimmed hat.

'What be happening?'

He looked up as Oneesha stepped to the bench carrying a bowl and piece of bread, the white apron covering her faded yellow dress stained by the morning's work. 'They done found Miss Lilly's body by the river,' he replied as she seated herself beside him and he glanced back, the men beginning to disperse in order to conduct their search for clues as to the murderer's identity.

'She was but nine years old.' Oneesha looked at him in disgusted shock.

He nodded as he regarded her warm features, gaze settling on her large eyes, irises a rich brown and lit by a kind intelligence. 'Have you done had time to think on what I say to you?' he asked.

She stared at her broth and frowned, Isaac looking at the soft pout of her lips in profile. 'Mayhap this not be the right time to be talking of it,' she replied in an attempt to evade the subject.

'I love you, Neesh. That be as true of this time as any other. I want to marry you,' he stated, laying his hand upon hers as it rested upon her knee and she clutched the bread.

She sighed and looked up at him regretfully. 'And if one of us be sold?'

'That be not happening,' he replied firmly.

'It be not your say so.' She looked at him regretfully.

'We run away.'

Oneesha shook her head. 'You know what happens when they be catching us,' she said, taking her hand from his and dipping the torn edge of her bread into the gruel,

3

letting the drips fall back into the bowl before taking a bite.

'Who say they catch us?' he asked as he continued to regard her with the intensity of his affection.

'Well, well, what do we have here?' said Silas as he swaggered around the corner of the women's cabin before them, the building no more than a long dilapidated shed mirroring the dormitory for the male slaves which rested at their backs.

'You be trying to get yourself a piece of tail, Isaac?' he asked with self-amusement, lop-sided grin upon his face as he came to a stop, left hand upon his hip and gun hand hanging loose by the holster.

'No, Sir,' he replied as he and Oneesha held their heads low, eyes to the ground and the farmhand's snakeskin boots.

'Ain't you s'pposed to be seeing to them horses?'

'Yessir. I just done finish eating,' Isaac replied with a nod as he got to his feet, holding the bowl in both hands.

'Then you better get to it unless you want to be feeling my boot on your backside.'

Isaac nodded again and made his way around the end of the bench, glancing back before entering the shadows of the male slave quarters and noting the leer on Silas' face as he looked down upon Oneesha.

'How you doing there, Little Missy?' asked the farmhand, moving to seat himself where Isaac had been sitting moments before.

Oneesha simply nodded, drawing her left arm tight to her body in an attempt to create some distance between them and keeping her gaze averted as she consumed the meagre meal.

'Taste good, does it?' Silas leant forward and sniffed the gruel before turning to look up at her face.

She gave another nod, feeling his gaze upon her and self-consciously drawing the collar of her dress together with her free hand.

'Now don't go getting all shy on me.' He reached over and cupped her chin, turning her head and raising her eyes to his. 'I bet you're a tasty little thing.'

Movement caught his eye and he looked up to find Isaac standing in the doorway to the men's cabin. 'What you looking at, nigger? Get to them horses or they'll be a spell in the hole for you.'

Isaac hesitated a moment and then made his way behind Oneesha, subtly stroking the faded cotton of her dress in a gesture of reassurance as he passed. Knowing

5

that Silas would be watching him, he resisted the urge to look back. He walked around the end of the slave quarters, feeling the palpable weight of the sun's merciless gaze.

Running a hand over his tightly cropped scalp as it itched with gathered grime, he made for the track and turned right. Heading north alongside the cluster of sheds and barns, he hoping the head farmhand would leave Oneesha in peace, the thought of him doing her harm bringing with it an increase in tension as he turned off towards the stables.

2

Oneesha walked through the long shadows of evening, pausing amidst the copse of trees between the cotton fields and the sheds. Spanish moss hung from the spreading branches in feathery stillness, the swing Miss Lilly had often used whispering of her demise and casting a shadow that reached further than any other.

Continuing beyond the trees, she passed across the dusty track beside the slave quarters and walked around the end of the men's cabin. Looking to the small area of wooden benches between the slave cabins, she found no one seated there, their work keeping them until later hours.

She glanced over at the bunkhouse, seeing one of the farmhands seated on the simple front porch smoking a cigarette. Wandering over to the women's dormitory, she stepped to the door set a few yards along its side.

Opening it to the creak of hinges, Oneesha entered the gloom, a scattering of rickety cots about the walls and two resting in the centre end to end. She padded up the first aisle, making her way to the far corner and stopping before her cot, a smile graced her lips as she looked at the pillow. An indentation had been lined with cotton and within the handmade nest rested a pair of eggs.

Noting a piece of sackcloth tucked beneath, she picked up the eggs to reveal a rough drawing of a tree with a half-moon above. She regarded it with her head cocked to one side, her smile broadening.

The door to the cabin opened behind her and Oneesha hastily slipped the eggs into the front pocket of her grubby apron. Gathering up the cotton and note, she hid them beneath the straw-filled pillow and straightened.

'You be done already?'

She turned to find Seyeh standing in the doorway, grasping the handle as she looked across the room. 'Yes,' she nodded.

'Then you can be helping me with the food,' stated the rotund woman, hair held in a deep blue cloth matching her dress.

Oneesha looked to her pillow to ensure that none of the cotton beneath could be seen and then made her way back along the length of the dormitory, Seyeh regarding her inquisitively as she approached.

'What he bring you this time?' she asked knowingly, seeing the brush of red upon the younger woman's cheeks and noting the down-turned gaze.

'Eggs,' admitted Oneesha, retrieving them from the pocket and holding them out as she came to a halt.

Seyeh surveyed them and then smiled. 'He be a good man, Neesh.'

'I know,' she replied, looking at the floorboards between them.

'Have you done made up your mind yet?'

Oneesha shook her head and lifted her gaze to the other woman. 'How can we be wed? This be no life for a husband and wife.'

Seyeh's smile softened. 'Marriage never be easy, slave or not,' she stated. 'Have I done told you I once had a husband?'

Oneesha's expression showed her surprise.

'His name be Manny. I weren't but fourteen and he a year older when we be wed.'

'What happened?'

Seyeh looked over her shoulder and then stepped into the cabin, Oneesha moving aside. The older woman closed the door and moved to sit on the nearest cot, the slats groaning their complaint. She sat a moment and then looked up, nodding towards the space beside her.

Oneesha seated herself, hands upon her lap and the eggs cradled upon her right palm.

'Manny were a hot head,' began Seyeh. 'He never take too kindly to being pushed around and when they be hiring a new hand who done a lot of pushing, things went bad,' she said with a shake of her head as she looked at the small shuttered window across from them.

'Otis be his name and he were a mean son of a bitch. He rode Manny like a trail horse. Sometimes he take it, others he didn't. The beatings and whippings never did much but feed his hate.'

'Were it Otis that done killed him?'

Seyeh turned to her and nodded. 'Manny bled out after Otis whipped him awful bad.'

'What happened to Otis?'

'Died from the fever not long afore you arrive, but his son be just as mean.'

'Silas?'

Seyeh nodded once again. 'You be watching out for that one, Neesh. One of the girls here be with child soon after Manny died and were strangled in her sleep. Folks say it were Otis and I say, like father like son.'

3

She glanced upward as the soundless shadow of an owl passed overhead, gliding the length of the meadow and lost to sight as it was masked by the dark woods at the far end. Arms out to the sides, Oneesha brushed the tall grasses beside her as she walked, dew kissing her fingers with cool tenderness. The sickle moon hung low and burnt orange in the sky, rising over the river, its shattered reflection dancing on the waters.

She approached the willow in her long and pale nightshirt, eyes wide as she sought her love beneath the boughs. Walking into the darkness, she moved to the trunk, right palm to its roughness as she stepped around, seeking him out, but finding nothing but shadows lurking on the other side.

'Isaac?' she whispered as loud as she dare, the hush demanding her respectful restraint.

A soft whistle sounded from above and gave her a start. Oneesha turned to find him seated on a branch fifteen feet from the ground, the moonlight hinting at his smile. 'What you be doing up there?'

'Waiting for you,' he replied, amusement in his tone.

Isaac slipped from the branch and landed beside her, straightening as he turned. 'Was you seen?' he asked.

'Seyeh be awake by the door, but she know we meet and know when to be holding her tongue,' she responded. 'She done boiled the eggs earlier and sneak them back to me in a handkerchief. I give one back. If you be caught stealing them it be the whipping post or hole for you.'

'I find them under a bush, not in the coop.'

'They still be calling it stealing.'

He nodded, the gesture almost lost in the gloom. Raising his hand to her cheek, he cradled it and stroked her skin with his thumb. 'Did he touch you?'

The question hung in the stillness a moment.

Oneesha shook her head. 'Seyeh called me up to the Big House to help with the sweeping. She seen us from a window.' She took his hand in hers, taking it from her cheek.

'She sets me to thinking of my ma,' she stated wistfully.

She looked out to the river, low mist building above the sluggish waters as they stood robed in thoughtful shadows. Their eyes glittered as the moon rose higher into the night sky and lost the stains of her birth, becoming pale and dusted.

Isaac gave her hand a gentle squeeze before seating himself beside the willow's broad trunk, drawing her down beside him. They settled with the rough bark at their backs, his arm passing about her shoulders as Oneesha rested her head against him.

'My ma done sung a song on dark and silent nights after my pa...' She struggled to put voice to the words. '...After he be gone,' she finished, softening the truth.

'Will you sing it to me?' asked Isaac, studying her contemplative expression as she continued to stare out at the meadow.

There was a short silence as she gathered the words, recalling her mother seated by the window, staring out at the night as if hoping for her pa's return.

'Willow, sweet willow, cry no tears for me, I'll be gone by sun-up, this rope will set me free. Willow, sweet willow, bow your head no more, the river banks are swollen, with tears I shed before.

'Mine has been a troubled life, they've hung me here to dry, the shackles no longer chain me down, there's no need to cry.

'Willow, sweet willow, cry no tears for me, I'll be gone by sun-up, this rope will set me free. Willow, sweet willow, bow your head no more, the river banks are swollen, with tears I shed before.

'This I say with my last breath, the Lord he waits for me, by His side I'll be no slave, so cry no tears for me.

'Willow, sweet willow, cry no tears for me, I'll be free by sun-up, this rope is liberty. Willow, sweet willow, bow your head no more, the river calls me onward, to a distant shore,' she finished, the pace of the last line having slowed and the last note held as it faded on her breath.

The silence pressed in, the tree at their backs briefly shivering as a breath of wind passed through the meadow, the rippling grasses marking its passage.

Isaac reached over and wiped a stray tear from Oneesha's cheek. 'Beautiful,' he whispered, describing more than just the song as he looked down upon her face, the haunting melody lingering in his mind.

She slowly turned to him and looked into his eyes as they leant close. Their lips met. Eyes closing and arms about each other, they savoured the brief taste of freedom, lost to the tenderness of the lasting embrace.

Oneesha eventually drew back from him and took hold of his hands. 'Yes,' she said softly, staring into his darkened eyes meaningfully.

A fleeting look of confusion was replaced by a smile as Isaac realised the question to which she was giving her answer. He squeezed her hands, the communication of their eyes needing no words as the willow at their backs creaked softly.

'We best go back before we be missed,' she stated, looking up at the moon through the branches.

'We could take to our feet? If we go now, we not be missed 'til dawn.'

'And then we be hunted down by dogs,' she responded, releasing his hands and getting to her feet.

'Not if we be swimming the river downstream,' he suggested.

'No one ever done taught me to swim,' she replied as she brushed down the back of her nightshirt.

'Then that be something need changing,' he stated with a smile.

Taking her hand, Isaac led her from beneath the boughs and into the grass. They moved through the mist, bare feet light upon the ground as they went to the riverside.

Arm brushing aside the bull rushes at the water's edge, Isaac brought them to a halt. The waters babbled against the bank as a wild cry arose from the concealing darkness of the woods on the far bank.

'We best go back,' reiterated Oneesha, looking to the ribbons of moonlight shifting upon the surface and not relishing the thought of entering the river's hidden depths.

Isaac released her hand and stripped off his leggings and shirt, standing naked before her.

'Now I be knowing why you think this a good idea,' she said with a raised eyebrow, a thin smile upon her lips.

He laughed and stepped down into the shallows with a gentle splash. Standing knee-deep, he held his hand out to her and beckoned. 'Come.'

Oneesha stared at him a moment before looking over her shoulder, seeing nothing but the mist moving above the meadow. Slipping the nightshirt from her shoulders, she let it tumble to her feet. She allowed his gaze to take in her nakedness, resisting the urge to cover herself with her hands.

He beckoned once again.

She stepped to the bank, feeling the pliant earth beneath her feet and looking nervously at the waters.

Isaac moved further out, the river quickly rising to his waist.

With a flutter in her stomach, Oneesha stretched out a foot to the rippling surface. She tentatively entered the river, a pensive expression on her face as she stood beside the security of the bank, feet sinking into the cool mud of the bed.

Isaac let himself fall back, arms to the sides and legs kicking out in front of him. 'Swim with me,' he requested, drifting further out, fingers of mist about his glistening shoulders.

She battled her fear and took another step as Isaac turned onto his front and began to swim upstream to the left. The disturbance of his activity washed against her thighs and caused hesitation, her nervousness rising in response to the unsettling movements.

He turned, swimming back towards her, moving closer to the bank.

Her heart leapt as the dark shape of a bird bolted from the reeds. It cried out in alarm, wings rapid in its sudden ascent.

Oneesha turned and climbed from the river, quickly gathering up her nightshirt.

17

'It be only a bird,' said Isaac as he stood within the waters and waded toward the bank, his nakedness dripping with captured moonlight.

'It be a sign. We must go back now, Isaac,' she said, looking about worriedly, uneasy and feeling the weight of time's passage, every moment they lingered bringing the possibility of discovery closer.

She raised the shirt and drew it over her head, freeing her hair with a shake of her head and the dampening cotton hiding her nakedness once more.

Isaac bent to the reeds beside him, plucking up a white handkerchief from between their stalks. 'You must have done dropped it when you be undressing,' he stated, holding it out to her as he rose from the water.

Oneesha stared at it and noted pale yellow flowers embroidered at the corners of its crumpled form. 'It not be mine.'

'It not be the one Seyeh used for the eggs?'

She shook her head.

He stood thoughtfully for a moment. 'Take it,' he said, holding it closer.

'But it not be mine,' she restated.

'It be no one's anymore and I be sure the river don't need it.' He smiled at her. 'It be fortune's gift, yours by happenstance.'

She reluctantly took the handkerchief, briefly studying the delicate flowers with green stems that grew inwards, her thumb running over one of them and feeling the rise of stitching. Isaac watched, smiling to himself before rinsing his feet in the river and dressing.

Oneesha tucked the handkerchief inside the top of her shirt, the quality of is soft cotton contrasting with the roughness of her night attire. She waited, keeping a watchful eye as Isaac pulled his shirt over his head and tugged the hem down.

They set off hand in hand, the grasses whispering against them. Leaving the meadow, they passed between the cotton fields beyond. The Big House came into view on the left, its whitewashed walls aglow and a film of translucent moonlight upon the windows.

Keeping low, they moved single-file between the rows of cotton plants in the large north field behind the house, Isaac taking the lead and filled with the heavy scent of fresh earth that would be beaten back when day came. Reaching the gateway, they quickly moved across the track that went east back towards the meadow, but which they chose to avoid when returning for fear of being spied upon its openness.

Making their way along the end of the cotton store, their presence was masked from the Big House by a small group of trees hung with washing lines to the left. They snuck by a small shed and made their way to the rear of the farmhand's bunkhouse. Drawing up to its slatted wall, they glanced around as they caught their breath, snores issuing from within.

Isaac moved to the corner and looked across the expanse of dusty yard to the slave quarters. He glanced over his shoulder, expression asking a silent question.

Oneesha nodded and moved to his side. Bracing herself with a deep breath, she ran fleet-footed across to the welcoming concealment afforded at the rear of the women's dormitory, Isaac watching her ghostly passage.

There was no call of alarm and he followed in haste, joining her before they moved to the far corner. He surveyed the space between the slave cabins, finding only darkened shadows gathered about the scattering of benches resting there.

'My turn,' he whispered.

He quickly made his way across the narrow yard, hunched and fearful. He reached the men's cabin and hugged the deep shadows, making his way past a couple of barrels set against the wall.

Moving by the benches, Isaac came upon the door and took hold of the handle. Turning, he raised his hand in silent farewell before entering to the wincing creak of hinges.

Crouching, Oneesha waited for any who may have stirred upon her entry to drift back into slumber. A cricket chirruped at the edge of her hearing, its rub interrupted by shifting in the bunk on the other side of the wooden slats, a groan arising before the noises ceased.

She rose and made her way along the length of the cabin. Arriving before the door at the far end, she paused, the hairs on the nape of her neck prickling.

She glanced back towards the bunkhouse porch, only its edge visible from her vantage point. Her gaze roamed further, settling on the raised grand porch of the Big House, but seeing only darkness behind its side railings as she looked along its span.

Oneesha took a breath and then entered the deep gloom of the dormitory.

A match flared behind the shelter of a cupped hand on the porch of the Big House. It lifted, illuminating Silas' face as he drew on the mouth of his pipe and the tobacco in its bowl glowed brightly, the match flames drawn town in the crackle of addiction's satisfaction.

With a flick of his wrist, the match was extinguished. Flicking its spent form over the end of the railings, he moved to sit on their edge, one boot to the floorboards as he looked towards the shack into which Oneesha had snuck.

He exhaled through his nose, the smoke hanging in the air momentarily before the breeze lifted again and ushered it into the night. The fumes coiled up the side of the porch roof, rising into the moonbeams.

With another thoughtful draw on the pipe, Silas grinned to himself, upper teeth glistening, eyes hidden in the shadow cast by the rim of his hat. The Spanish moss stirred in the trees which stood on the far side of the north track from the buildings, the empty swing rocking as if a spirit rested upon its seat, ropes creaking gently.

4

The heads of the pickaxes dug into the baked earth at the base of the tree trunk. Isaac raised his in the air once again as Anthony paused to wipe his brow with his forearm. They stood in the recently cleared west field, a small plot of land at the fringe of the plantation. The trees had fallen to the axe the previous week, the lumber piled against the stone wall to the sides of the gateway. Wilson reclined on one of the piles, hat slipped over his face, shotgun resting on his lap at the foot of his substantial belly and horse standing motionless nearby.

Anthony began to toil once again, the trunks scattered about the field speaking of the work still to come. 'We could be doing with more help,' he muttered without turning, 'it be taking weeks to dig these out.'

Isaac nodded, sweat dripping from his face and adding a fading touch of darkness to the soil at his feet. His shirt clung to his back and the odour of his body filled his nostrils as he worked to brake up the soil. 'Where was you Monday afternoon?' he asked as he swung the pickaxe and it thumped into the ground, the question having been lingering for two days.

'What be your meaning?'

'I done looked for you, but found no sign.' Isaac glanced over, seeing tightness about the other man's eyes that betrayed his tension.

'I be tending the horses,' Anthony replied after a moment.

'Was you hiding?' asked Isaac as he paused, leaning on the head of the pickaxe.

Anthony looked at him in confusion.

'I looked in, but done found no one in the stables.'

'I be in the paddock, not the stables.' Anthony beat the earth with greater vigour.

Isaac watched a moment and then set to the task again, fully aware that none of the horses had been out to grass that afternoon. 'I be saying nothing to no one,' he said in reassurance.

'Because there be nothing to say,' responded Anthony with annoyance, the perspiration upon his face highlighting the scarring about his left eye from one of the numerous beatings he'd received in the past.

'Less talking, more digging,' called Silas as he rode up to the gateway, Wilson stirring and hastily sitting up as he slid his hat back onto his head, the gun nearly slipping from his grasp.

'Ain't getting enough sleep?' asked Silas as he looked down at the farmhand.

Wilson didn't respond as he struggled to his feet with a groan, disturbing the logs and one tumbling to the ground, a small plume of dust rising. He scratched at his grizzly beard, hair catching under his dirty fingernails as he looked over at the two slaves working in the field.

'Mr Canyon wants them stumps out by the end of the week.' Silas lifted the brim of his hat and wiped his brow.

Wilson turned to him, an expression of stupefaction on his rounded face. 'That ain't possible unless you send on over more help.'

'Maybe you should be working them niggers harder instead of catching winks.'

'I ain't been asleep more than a couple of minutes,' he responded defensively.

Silas glanced at the two slaves, their pickaxes rising and falling in a steady rhythm. 'I'll talk to Mr Canyon and see if there's any to spare.'

Wilson nodded, waving away a fly. 'Another half dozen should do it.'

'Half dozen!' scoffed Silas, shaking his head. 'Now I know you be dreaming. Mr Canyon has most of the men digging a new irrigation ditch and he won't be sparing them for the likes of this,' he said, nodding towards the field and watching the work for a moment.

'Waste good time talking again and it'll be time in the hole for you,' he called out.

Isaac and Anthony continued to beat out their working rhythm.

'You hear me, niggers?'

'Yessir,' replied Isaac with a nod, knowing that if he were to turn he would be reprimanded for not paying attention to the task.

He glanced over at Anthony when no response was forthcoming from him, seeing the scowl upon his face as he swung his pickaxe with greater vigour. He'd only been at the plantation for a couple of months and spoke nothing of his past, but it whispered upon his face and in the lash marks that lay across his back.

Isaac resisted the urge to turn as he heard the horse approach at a slow gait, not wishing to give Silas any excuse to exercise his idea of justice. The mount was brought to halt behind them and whinnied in the brief silence that followed.

'You hear me, Anthony?' asked Silas, voice low and threatening.

'Yessir,' he replied, the word laced with disdain.

Isaac tensed as he blinked away sweat that ran into his eyes, not daring to pause even to clear his stinging sight.

'I've heard about you, boy,' stated Silas. 'You bit off a man's ear over in Opelousas.'

Anthony didn't respond, his pickaxe rising and falling.

'Did you hear what I say, nigger?'

'Yessir.'

'You be trying anything like that here, you'll be sorry the Lord ever saw fit to give you breath. You understand me?'

'Yessir.'

Silas remained behind them, the tension palpable as the pickaxes thudded against the hardened ground, beating out time.

'You want to watch this one,' called Silas over his shoulder before clicking his tongue twice in close succession and kicking his heels against the horse's flanks.

The creature turned and made its way back to the entrance of the field. Isaac wiped his eyes with the back of his hand, the dust that had gathered there smearing

27

across the bridge of his nose and muddying in the perspiration. He glanced at Anthony as they continued to work.

'Say nothing.' The words were an unfriendly growl.

'Either of these niggers gives you any trouble and send them straight to the hole,' stated Silas as he passed through the gateway.

'Be sure you talk with Mr Canyon,' said Wilson.

'And you be sure you don't go catching anymore winks on me,' replied Silas as he gave the reins a snap and the horse picked up its speed, trotting into the adjacent cotton field.

5

Oneesha knelt by the river amidst the line of five women, scrubbing boards against their knees and clothes bunched in their raw hands. They rocked back and forth as they rubbed the washing, pausing to dunk it into the waters and wring it out from time to time.

'I done see Miss Lilly's body this morning,' stated Mitilde, who was barely sixteen and had only been at the plantation for a year. 'She lying in the second drawing room in an open casket,' she added as she knelt to the right of the group.

'What you be doing in the second drawing room?' asked Seyeh, turning to the young slave.

She blushed in response.

'I thought as much.'

'I was curious is all.'

'I hope none of the white folks done saw you.' Seyeh regarded her closely.

Mitilde shook her head, leaning forward to dip the shirt she was holding into the river, the stains upon the collar deeply ingrained and proving hard to rub away.

The women worked wordlessly for a while, baskets resting in the grasses beside them.

'She were awful cold,' stated Mitilde, who often found silence to be a burden she could not bear.

The other women looked to her in surprise, Seyeh falling still.

'You touched Miss Lilly?'

Mitilde turned to the collective stares and then averted her gaze. 'Only a little, with the backs of my fingers,' she replied. 'She look so peaceful, like she were but sleeping,' she added by way of explanation for her actions.

Seyeh glanced over her left shoulder, looking to the willow fifty yards away. Their chaperone was seated beneath as his horse grazed on the grasses.

'You should not be a sneaking around the Big House, Mitty,' she admonished, turning back to the girl. 'Any of the white folks see you and it be time in the hole for sure, if not worse.'

'I be careful.'

'Careful or not, you catch a hiding if you be caught,' said Angie, seated between and pausing to adjust the peach coloured binding about her hair.

'You go nowhere in the Big House unless you has reason to be going there, you understand?' said Seyeh firmly.

Mitilde nodded, her head bowed.

'The white folks don't take too kindly to us being where we got no cause to be,' said Seyeh with a softer tone, 'and I not be wanting you to suffer the lash.'

Mitilde gave another nod and began to rub the shirt on the board leaning before her, her demeanour one of dejection. Seyeh watched her for a moment and then continued with her own scrubbing, water seeping over her reddened fingers as she squeezed the cotton.

'I see Mistress Canyon this morning,' stated Venus, who was seated to the far left of the group. 'She were head to toe in black and her face veiled.'

'Miss Lilly's death is awful burdensome,' said Seyeh. 'She done stayed in her room until today,' she added, all the women aware that their Master and Mistress slept in separate rooms.

'She were wandering the Big House like a ghost. I be coming out the kitchens and caught myself a fright upon seeing her in the dining room. She were stroking the cloth where Miss Lilly used to sit. I be wishing her good day, but she drift away without a word.'

'Who could be doing such a terrible thing?' asked Mitilde with a shake of her head.

Seyeh sighed. 'She were a sweet child.'

'One time she offer me to help clear the table,' said Venus with a nod. 'I would have let her but for the beating that would have been my reward for not attending my duties right.'

'It must be the same one killed her as killed before,' said Angie.

'They be saying so,' nodded Seyeh.

They all glanced over at the woods on the far bank where the body of a woman from Bayou Chene had been found beaten and strangled.

'They both be abiding with the Lord now,' stated Seyeh.

'Amen,' said Venus with a nod.

There were a few moments of silence as they set to the washing once again.

'Casius say Master Canyon sent for someone from Attakapas County,' commented Mitilde.

'I hear the same, someone from Vermilionville,' concurred Angie with a nod.

'Someone?' asked Oneesha.

'An investigator,' clarified Angie.

'If there be no clues then there be nothing to investigate,' said Seyeh.

The women all pondered as they rubbed the clothes on their boards.

'They be finding nothing?' asked Mitilde.

'Only Miss Lilly's red coat lying sorrowful in the rushes,' replied Seyeh.

Mitilde looked fearfully along the bank to her right, seeing a moorhen between the stalks. 'Were she found close by?'

'Now don't be getting yourself all stirred up. Set your mind to your washing.'

Mitilde shifted, shoulders trembling as a shiver passed through her. Oneesha looked over and saw the girl's uneasiness, the feeling settling upon her as if contagious. She glanced at the rushes, an image coming to mind of the girl lying in the waters like a discarded rag doll, bedraggled and pale-faced as she stared sightlessly at the sky.

Her pulse increased and she took a breath.

'They say the smell of the river still be holding onto her,' stated Venus.

'What you be wagging about now?' asked Angie.

'Miss Lilly. I hear tell they wash her over and over, but the river won't leave her be.'

'I could smell it,' nodded Mitilde.

'Some folks say the river has a spirit that whispers. Those that be hearing it are called to its waters,' said Venus.

Seyeh nodded. 'And some folks say that if tongues done stopped their wagging then such fancies would never be given breath.'

'It be true, Seyeh,' stated Angie. 'There be a voice to these here waters. You remember when Old Tarbuck drowned himself. They said he just upped and walked out of the bunkhouse like he were dreaming.'

'When that be?' asked Mitilde, staring at Angie in fearful enthralment.

'A few years back. He were called to the river. It took his spirit, like it has taken Miss Lilly's.'

'Her death be no drowning. She were killed,' stated Seyeh with increasing frustration, not one to hold with superstition.

'Mayhap the killer heard the whisper,' said Venus. 'The river talks to the darkness in men's souls, for it be souls upon which it feeds.'

'We be hearing no more of this foolish talk,' said Seyeh dismissively as she rubbed grey leggings upon her board with increased agitation.

'It feeds on souls?' Mitilde looked at the waters before her, the light dancing on the ripples reflected in her wide eyes.

'You got cotton in them there ears? I says, no more,' snapped Seyeh, turning to the girl. 'Get to your work, Mitty, and be mindful you do it well. I want no more stains left on forgotten cuffs.'

Tension hung in the air as they continued with the washing. Oneesha glanced along the line, seeing the tightness of expressions and stiff postures. Seyeh was beating and rubbing the stains from the clothes as if their presence caused great offence, her heated actions adding to the oppressive wordlessness.

She began to hum *Willow, Sweet Willow*, hopeful that the tune would alleviate the pressure.

'Hum it again, Neesh,' said Angie when the tune came to an end, the women's shoulders loosened by the gentle melody and Seyeh's movements having calmed.

Oneesha hummed the song for a second time, rubbing a pale shirt against her board as she did so. As the last sounds left her lips, a bright blue dragonfly settled on the bank beside her, the sunlight shimmering upon its veined wings.

She studied it, noting the bulbous eyes that appeared to be regarding her. Reaching out with her index finger, she made to touch it.

The dragonfly took to the sky, the sound of its wings like dried leaves rattling against a stem.

'That be a sign,' said Venus as Oneesha watched the insect pass over the waters.

'Of what?' she asked, turning to the other woman.

'That change be a coming. Change and transformation.'

Seyeh laughed derisively. 'Change always be a coming. That be one of the few things you can rely on in this here life.'

Venus gave her a hard look as they scrubbed. 'You mark my words. There be change in your life and that real soon,' she whispered after a while, Seyeh glancing over and shaking her head.

They finished the washing and took up the baskets, heavier now that they were filled with damp clothing.

Jerry was already upon his mount, rifle resting across the pommel of the saddle as he watched them lift their burdens.

They followed the horse in a staggered line, the beast at an easy walk as it made its way along the meadow. Oneesha walked at the back, enjoying the sensation of the ground against her bare feet and glancing back at the willow, smiling to herself as she thought of Isaac.

Seyeh slowed her pace, drawing alongside her and giving her a look to indicate they should drop back from the others. Oneesha's stride lessened and the yards drew out between them and Mitilde.

'And?' asked the older woman quietly, adjusting her hold on the basket upon her shoulder.

Oneesha immediately knew what she was referring to. 'I say yes to him this last night,' she replied with a coy smile and a slight blush.

Seyeh nodded. 'You be a good match and I am glad,' she stated. 'When will you be wed?'

'We not speak on it yet.'

Seyeh nodded, glancing ahead before speaking again. 'You must be careful, Neesh. Many are the tongues that wag when things are seen, especially things secret.'

Oneesha nodded. 'We only be meeting at the willow one or two times a week,' she replied, looking back at the tree at they began to file out of the meadow.

Seyeh followed her gaze.

'Are you two fixing to join us?' called Jerry.

They looked ahead to find the farmhand staring at them, turned in the saddle.

'Yessir,' replied Seyeh, beginning to walk faster.

Oneesha shifted the weight of her basket as Seyeh moved before her. They made their way between the cotton fields, a smile upon her face as she thought about the answer she had given to Isaac, knowing that it reflected the feelings held within her heart.

6

Oneesha and Seyeh hung the washing out on lines strung between the trees edging the back lawn of the Big House, a small shed on the far side and the large barn of the cotton store rising behind it. The other women had been dismissed and Jerry had been assigned to the cotton fields. They were alone with the billowing sheets and clothing.

'Tomorrow we be washing the household linens,' stated Seyeh.

Oneesha nodded as she looked at the shirt she'd hung, pulling it to the right so as to draw out the wrinkles where it bunched. She didn't mind washing the household linens and clothes from the Big House so much. It was done in large tin tubs on the back lawn with fragranced soaps and she always enjoyed the scent lingering on her hands.

'Will you be meeting Isaac tonight?' asked Seyeh as she bent to retrieve a pair of leggings, glancing at Oneesha opposite her as she puffed with the effort, her increasingly rotund figure making the work tiresome.

She shrugged. 'It be not often two nights in a row.'

'But you wish it were so.' The older woman smiled warmly.

Oneesha looked down at the basket at her feet with abashment. 'I wish it were so every night.'

'That be love, girl,' chuckled Seyeh.

Oneesha looked up. 'What do we do with it?' she asked, her words with a pleading tone as she sought an answer.

'I be lost to your meaning.'

'What do we do with love when we be but slaves?'

Seyeh nodded in understanding. 'You savour it. You gain strength to endure from it. You remember every moment together.' She sighed and looked along the line of swaying washing that she'd already hung, gaze moving to the Big House.

'Most of all, you look into his eyes and forget you be a slave,' she added softly, recalling her lost love.

Oneesha studied her fallen expression. 'My pardon,' she said, feeling guilty for having stirred the pain that lingered.

Seyeh turned back to her. 'There be nothing you need pardoning for, Neesh. I be glad for what I had. When he done held me in his arms and I looked into his eyes...'

40

She shook her head and took another breath. 'Love as a slave be a taste of freedom.'

'I bitter taste?'

'Bittersweet,' replied Seyeh with a sad smile and nod. 'Come, let's be finishing up and get to the cooking.' She bent with a slight groan and picked out a dress, reaching up to hang it over the line.

Oneesha took up the last garment, glancing to the full basket of washing resting beneath the tree to her right. Her sight was attracted by movement on the far side of the Big House and the hairs on her arms rose and tingled in response to what she saw.

'Seyeh,' she whispered, nodding towards the unsettling sight when the older woman looked over at her.

They watched as Mistress Canyon walked through the grove of widely spaced persimmons. She was coming along the central avenue pushing a large and dusty perambulator, talking to the emptiness that Oneesha knew lay within and pausing to rock it on rusted springs.

'That be Miss Lilly's from when she were but a babe,' commented Seyeh.

Oneesha simply nodded, watching as the gaunt figure swathed in black walked around the end of the avenue and began to walk away along the next.

41

'She be greatly disturbed by the loss,' said the older woman with a sorrowful shake of her head as she turned back to the clothes line before her.

Oneesha found it hard to tear her gaze away, spellbound by the unnatural sight as Mistress Canyon drew to a halt and bent forward, speaking into the vacancy before her and then laughing.

'Neesh,' hissed Seyeh, looking to the right meaningfully.

Oneesha blinked, freeing herself from the eerie enchantment and glancing in the direction the older woman had indicated. Silas was watching them as he stood beside the rear of the farmhand's bunkhouse. He raised his hand and touched the brim of his hat, his lopsided grin broad as he leant against the slats.

She turned away, taking up the empty basket by her feet and stepping to the tree where the full one rested in waiting. Glancing across the lawn at the persimmon grove, she could still make out the black figure of Mistress Canyon. She was lingering on the far side, the branches masking her presence to a degree, the edges of the leaves curled and browned as the trees began to fruit.

7

The evening shadows were creeping across the yard as she made her way to the slave quarters. She went into the female cabin, finding no one else present. Moving through the stale heat gathered from the passing day, Oneesha went to her cot, looking to the pillow as she walked across the room, but seeing no evidence of Isaac having visited.

Halting before the bed, she lifted the end of the cover despite knowing that he always left his gifts upon the pillow. Feeling disappointed, she seated herself. She had not seen him all day, one of the other women saying that he'd been put to work in the west field.

Soft scraping drew her gaze to the slatted shutters to her left. Rising, she stepped over and peered through one of gaps to the dusty window pane beyond. A butterfly fluttered in the slanting sunlight, wings brushing the slats.

Oneesha watched for a few moments, the insect's vibrant colours indicating its recent emergence from a cocoon. She took in the swathes of burnt orange that brightly decorated its inner wings, the tips black and speckled with white.

Putting a hand to the bottom of the shutters, she raised them and took the butterfly into the cage of her fingers, feeling its wings beat delicately against her skin. Letting them fall back into place, she gave the creature carriage through the dormitory, stepping out into the fading sunlight.

Unfurling her fingers, she watched as it slowly flexed it wings, waiting with expectation for it take flight and find liberty. The butterfly fluttered, lifting off her palm and then settling again, wings wide as it basked in the golden light.

Oneesha smiled, the sparkle in her eyes showing her delight. The breeze lifted and it took to the wing, flitting about her head momentarily and lifting into the sky. She shaded her eyes as the creature flew towards the sitting sun, her smile becoming melancholic.

'Change and transformation,' she mumbled to herself, remembering Venus' words upon the river bank.

8

The sound of crickets marked their exit from the field, the gateway dappled in the long shadows of the trees marking the boundary between the recently cleared land and scrub beyond. Isaac's body ached and his legs were leaded. He shuffled beside Anthony, Wilson riding ahead of them as the weak sunlight lay on their backs and they moved out between the cotton fields.

He felt the throb of blisters on the palm of his hand as he rested the pickaxe upon his shoulder. Anthony had suggested leaving the tools against the wall in readiness for the following day, but Wilson had reprimanded him, saying that he knew his job well enough and that no slave should be advising him.

The Big House came into sight beyond the collection of cabins and sheds gathered on its western side. They passed the small group of trees where the Spanish moss hung still and turned right onto the north-south track, walking along the barren earth towards the slave quarters.

'You boys go and get washed up now,' said Wilson, bringing his mount to a halt and turning to them.

'Yessir,' nodded Isaac.

'Yessir,' said Anthony without looking up.

'We'll be starting early or there ain't no chance of getting them trunks up by week's end.'

Isaac nodded again.

Wilson clicked his tongue and guided his horse towards the stables that lay to the rear of the collection of buildings.

'"We'll be staring early",' quoted Anthony under his breath, glaring at the farmhand's back. 'He ain't lifted but a finger.'

'Mayhap we be having more help when the new day comes,' said Isaac as they began to make their way over to the first of the cabins where the male slaves spent their nights.

Anthony looked at him without kindness. 'You be foolin' yourself,' he stated simply.

They walked around the end of the cabin and passed the group of benches between the two dormitories, going to a pair of water barrels resting in the shadows gathered between the buildings.

Isaac stepped up to one as Anthony hesitated, glancing around surreptitiously. Gathering up the cool water in his palms, Isaac closed his eyes and plashed it upon his face.

He was suddenly gripped firmly by the arm. Anthony turned him and took hold of the collar of his shirt, pushing him back against the cabin wall.

'Say one word of what you done heard and you be answering to me.'

Isaac blinked water from his eyes and stared at Anthony in shock. 'I be saying nothing,' he replied.

'Not even to your honey.'

Isaac shook his head.

'Be sure you don't.' Anthony gave him a shove, releasing him as he did so. Pausing, he then stepped over to the far barrel and began to strip off his shirt.

Isaac remained by the slats, taken aback by the unexpected threat. His gaze fell on the crosshatch of raised scars revealed upon Anthony's back and he realised how deep they ran. He looked to Anthony's dripping profile and wondered to what lengths he would go to satisfy his loathing of the white folk. He suspected much, but could prove nothing, and even if there were proof, could he in all honesty reveal the truth knowing what fate would befall his brother?

Isaac looked to the cabin opposite him, wishing he could see Oneesha. He ached for the depths of her eyes and the feel of her closeness as she rested in his arms, but there would be little or no contact while the clearance of the stumps kept him in the west field.

Frowning, he moved to the near barrel, Anthony ignoring his presence. Taking off his shirt, he began to wash away the dust and sweat of the day.

9

It was mid-morning and the heat of the day was already subduing the plantation. Oneesha and Seyeh sat before tin washing tubs that they'd brought out from the Big House and placed on the back lawn. The water was frothed by suds and the gentle scent of lilac lifted to them as their scrubbing boards leant against the near rims.

Oneesha took a white shirt from the water and inspected it, paying special attention to the collar and cuffs. Satisfied with its cleanliness, she wrung it tight, glittering streams of water forced from the cotton and falling back into the tub. Placing it in one of two baskets to her left, she then lifted the next garment to be washed from the other, pausing as she held it up before her.

She glanced to the persimmon grove as she lowered the child's blouse, the avenues between the boughs empty. Taking it beneath the water, she was reminded of how Miss Lilly had been found, the river whispering at the back of her mind.

Oneesha's brow furrowed as she scrubbed. She cocked her head to one side, sure she could hear the distant sound of men singing in the hot stillness. 'You be hearing that?' she asked, looking to the right in search of the source, but seeing nothing of note by the bunkhouse.

Seyeh stopped and listened for a few moments, her hands remaining in the water. 'It be men singing Dixie,' she said with a puzzled look as the voices drew closer, emanating from the far side of the Big House.

Rising, Seyeh grimaced and briefly placed her hands to her lower back. She began to make for the right-hand corner of the house with a waddling gait, Oneesha getting to her feet and following, the pale blouse left floating beneath the suds.

They passed along the side of the building and came to a stop when they reached the front, Oneesha peering over the older woman's shoulder with a touch of apprehension.

'There's buck-wheat cakes and Injun batter, makes you fat or a little fatter, look away, look away, look away, Dixie Land,' sung the small column of mounted soldiers, a confederate flag hanging limp in the stillness as it was borne at the head.

'Then hoe it down an' scratch your gravel, to Dixie's Land I'm bound to travel, look away, look away, look away, Dixie Land.'

Master Canyon walked from the double doors and onto the porch, coming to a stop at the top of the steps and leaning on his pale cane. He wore a dark cotton suit of mourning, his Stetson in stark contrast with his white hair, a single shot of black running down the centre of his angular beard.

The Captain raised his hand in the air, bringing the men to a stop and the song to a premature end. 'A fine good morning to you, Sir,' he greeted as his horse halted a few yards from the porch steps and he touched the brim of his hat in greeting. 'My name is Captain J.F. Harris.'

Master Canyon tapped the front of his hat with his index finger. 'John Canyon. What can I do for you boys?' he asked as Oneesha and Seyeh watched from beside the house, a number of the farmhands drifting closer from the buildings to the right, Silas amongst them.

'I would speak with you and hope to enjoy some southern hospitality.'

'About the war?'

Captain Harris glanced around, noting Oneesha and Seyeh's presence, his gaze then briefly settling on a figure veiled in black standing in the high corner window, brow furrowing for a moment before he turned his attention back to his host. 'It would be best if we spoke inside, if that be of no inconvenience. My men will remain, but I would appreciate some water for the horses.'

Canyon looked at the column of soldiers and then turned to the farmhands. 'Silas, fetch water for these horses and be sure to make sure these fine men are given refreshments.'

'Much obliged,' said Harris, touching the brim of his hat once again before dismounting.

'I better be going in,' stated Seyeh quietly, stepping back and turning to Oneesha.

'Where be Rose?' she asked as the older woman checked the state of her dress and the pale apron tied about her weighty hips.

Seyeh looked up, expression darkening. She glanced at the farmhands and soldiers before drawing Oneesha a few steps along the side of the house so they were hidden from sight. 'I done gave Rose the day to rest.'

Oneesha looked at her questioningly.

'She be bleeding,' she said with a downward glance, 'and there be bruises about her arms where she were held down.' Seyeh's gaze spoke of what went unsaid.

'Who?' whispered Oneesha, sickened by the thought of what had happened.

'She hold her tongue, but when I said Silas' name there were a flicker I did not miss.'

Oneesha glanced towards the front of the house, unable to see the head farmhand as he saw to watering the horses.

'I think he done took her as she changed the bed sheets yesterday.' Seyeh shook her head. 'She be but a sweet and innocent girl.'

Oneesha nodded, her stomach churning. Rose served in the Big House and so their paths rarely crossed. Despite their few encounters, she knew Rose to be timid, her slight figure and small voice accentuating her nature.

'Be there nothing to be done?' she asked.

'By who?' Seyeh looked at her meaningfully.

'But surely…'

'Neesh,' she interrupted with sad regret, 'there be nothing else to be done. If Silas has taken fancy to her we best be praying the Lord gives her strength to bear that cross.'

Oneesha looked to the ground, frustrated by the injustice and feeling the weight of their slavery.

Seyeh placed a hand upon her shoulder. 'One day we be free,' she comforted, 'and that day come when we walk through the gates of Heaven or when the Lord sees fit to open the hearts of the white folk.'

Oneesha nodded.

'How do I look?' Seyeh removed her hand and glanced down at herself again.

Oneesha looked her up and down, reaching out and tucking a lock of dark hair beneath the pale blue cloth tied about her head. 'There,' she said, attempting a smile, but her eyes betraying its lie.

Seyeh held her gaze a moment, heart reaching out to the young woman. 'You had better to the washing,' she said.

She nodded her response.

The two women returned to the rear of the house and gave nods of parting, Seyeh hurrying to the back entrance used by the slaves. Oneesha paused, watching her go to their Master's beck and call before walking back to the tub at which she'd previously been seated.

Her gaze fell on the blouse resting within, the suds gathered at the water's edge. Stepping around to face the Big House, she knelt on the short grass and was filled with a profound melancholy.

Reaching her hands into the water, she raised the blouse and wrung its sorrowful form. Taking it to the washing board, she began to hum *Willow, Sweet Willow,* eyes glistening with tears.

10

They sat in the thin shade afforded by the wall, their legs bathed in sunlight as they leant against the stones. Isaac turned to the pail between them, lifting the metal ladle and drinking down the water contained within as he glanced at Anthony, Wilson reclining on the far pile of lumber beyond the slave.

They had been sent no help and the morning had passed without a word being exchanged, the regular beat of the pickaxes the only sound as they broke up the ground about each stump in turn in readiness to hack and lever them out. Venus had brought the pail to the field just before noon, along with a parcel of bread and cheese.

Placing the hook of the ladle's handle over the side of the metal bucket, Isaac took up the stale bread and bit into it, the brittle crust scraping his gums. Chewing, he raised the cheese, a thin layer of white mould lending it a pungent aroma. He took a bite, looking out across the small field to the trees on the far side, watching as flies passed through the heat haze, their presence highlighted by the sunlight upon their wings.

Wrapping the remainder of his food in the grubby cloth in which it had been delivered, Isaac rested it at the foot of the wall to his right, knowing that he'd be in need of further sustenance as the day progressed. He was certain the work would continue well into the evening, as it had the day before and would for the foreseeable future.

He scanned the soil nearby and picked up a couple of twigs. Breaking off a stalk of tall grass from where it wilted beside the wall, he used it to tie them together in a cross.

Resting it upon his lap, Isaac searched for another twig. Finding one, he snapped it in two and bound the pieces to the near end, creating a simple stick figure. He smiled to himself as an idea came to him, his gaze seeking out additional small lengths of wood.

Anthony snorted and he turned to find him shaking his head and sneering.

'What?' he asked quietly, glancing at Wilson, who was chewing on a piece of salted pork rind and paying them no heed.

'Be you so blind to the truth?'

Isaac looked at him without comprehension.

57

'You be a slave that hides his eyes.'

'My eyes be open,' stated Isaac, 'and I see there be good to be found in this life.'

'Good!' scoffed Anthony, his voice briefly growing in volume. 'You be a fool.'

'No fool, but a slave who knows when fortune be in my favour,' replied Isaac softly. 'Master Canyon be giving us liberties that many of our people do not have and this life be better than one in the mines to the west.'

'You weigh two evils against each other. Canyon ain't no different from any other white folk.' There was fire in his eyes as his passion rose.

'Mayhap you think we should cut their throats as they sleep?' responded Isaac, leaning over the pail to ensure there was no chance of Wilson overhearing his seditious words.

Anthony remained silent, his brows lifting in suggestion of agreement.

'Time to get back to work, boys,' stated Wilson, punctuating his announcement with a burp and patting his sizeable stomach.

Isaac held Anthony's gaze a moment longer and then turned to the stick figure upon his lap, his sight settling on the bonds of grass. With a frown, he picked it up and

58

stood it against the stones beside the parcel of food before rising to his feet and making his way back to the tree stumps.

11

Seyeh looked out from the door of the women's cabin. The sky above was a deep purple chased westward by inky blue as night set in.

Stepping out, she moved to the corner on her left and peered round. There was no sign of anyone afore the Big House and she nodded over her shoulder, quickly departing the building and making her way across the ground to the men's cabin with Oneesha and Venus hurrying at her back.

They slunk in as quietly as they could, the hinges announcing their arrival with soft moans.

'What you be doing here?' asked Casius from his cot beside the door, looking up at them as he lay atop his covers in a pair of dark leggings, perspiration visible upon his chest despite the gloom.

'I be needing to speak with you all,' stated Seyeh, looking around the dormitory as the men stirred, turning to the disturbance or sitting up on their beds.

Casius looked from her face to those of the two women accompanying her, seeing expressions of excited secrecy. He swung his legs over the side and planted his bare feet on the floor. 'What be the need?'

Seyeh moved further into the room as Oneesha and Venus stayed by the door. She crouched amidst the gathered cots, looking about at the curious and weary faces and noting that Anthony remained watchful on the other side of the room.

'Have you all done heard about the soldiers that came a calling today?' she asked, keeping her voice low.

There was a round of nods, one of the younger slaves named Oscar stifling a yawn.

'Be there news of the war?' asked Isaac.

She nodded. 'They say it goes well.'

'Then what be the reason for their visit?' asked Casius.

'They ask Master Canyon if there be any men he can spare to enlist.'

'They seek more soldiers and yet say the war be going well?'

She nodded. 'But that be not why I need speak with you,' said Seyeh with a touch of impatience.

'What have you to say then?' enquired Casius.

'There be talk of the Union freeing slaves.'

61

There was a stunned silence, the men staring at her as the words sank in and a few glances passing between them in the growing darkness.

'You heard this?' asked Isaac, barely daring to believe it could be true.

Seyeh nodded. 'I done serve Master Canyon and the Captain. After taking them drinks and eats, I leant my ear to the door.'

'Be it certain?' asked Cesar as he leant forward, his grey beard speaking of the many years he'd spent under the yoke.

'I say only what I be hearing,' she replied.

'Did you hear more?'

She shook her head. 'One of the hands came into the kitchens and done called me in, asking for bread and cheese for the soldiers.'

'Where was Rose?' enquired Casius.

Seyeh glanced back at Oneesha. 'She been taken ill and took her rest for the day.'

'Freedom,' whispered Cesar, looking at the slats of the window opposite him and shaking his head in disbelief. 'I be thinking I find myself in the grave afore that day come.'

'You may still,' commented Anthony from the deep shadows on the far side of the room.

The slaves turned to him as he leant against the wall while sitting on his cot. 'You think if freedom be granted it be a lasting one? It be done to win the war and when that war is over slaves we be again.'

'There be no way for you to be sure of it,' said Cesar.

'As sure as I am of the sun rising when morning comes.'

A thoughtful hush filled the room as Seyeh's revelation was pondered by all present, its fertile hope woven with the seeds of Anthony's doubt. Cesar's bed creaked as he sat back and scratched at his bread, the sound loud in the stillness.

'We must be getting back to the cabin,' said Seyeh eventually, rising with a grunt and wince, arthritic pain in her knees flaring.

She walked over to the door, Oneesha and Venus parting. Opening it, she peered towards the Big House, finding no evidence of activity.

Isaac looked to Oneesha meaningfully and she gave an almost imperceptible nod in response.

'Come,' whispered Seyeh over her shoulder, the women quickly departing and the door closing on the night.

'What should we do?' asked Casius after a moment.

'Do?' Cesar looked over at him questioningly.

'What be there to do?' said Anthony.

'We could run to the north,' suggested Ben, cheeks sunken and stomach engorged by the worms with which he suffered due to his care of the hounds.

'Do you know how far that be?' responded Cesar. 'My age be not so able as yours.'

'We must do something,' said Isaac.

'There be only one thing we can but do. We wait for the war to end and pray to the Blessed Lord that the Union be the side victorious,' replied the old slave.

'*If* they grant freedom and *if* that freedom lasts when the fighting be over,' stated Oscar, Anthony's scepticism having taken root.

No words were offered to the cabin's interior as the men slowly settled down to rest. Despite their tiredness, many did not find sleep coming easily, turning time and again as their thoughts were disturbed by what had been said.

Isaac lay on his side staring at the wall before him. He listened to the creaking of cots, a groan or snore occasionally rising. He waited for the work of the day passed to take its toll on the others and his opportunity to vacate the cabin in order to meet with Oneesha, all the time pondering the prospect of liberty and the idea of fleeing to the north.

12

He was beginning to become agitated as he paced back and forth beneath the willow. He'd expected to find Oneesha in the deep shadows upon his arrival, such had been the wait for his departure from the cabin to become prudent, but she was not to be found.

Isaac stared along the meadow, glancing up at the thick cloud drawing in from the south, the promise of rain hanging in the stillness. His gaze scanned the rise that led to the cotton fields, wondering whether he should venture back.

An indistinct touch of paleness moved through the grasses like a spirit drifting into the meadow.

He stepped to the edge of the overhanging branches, narrowing his eyes. The beat of his heart gained in strength as the figure of his love gained definition. She swept towards him on swift feet, relief and longing drawing him out from beneath the willow, striding to meet her.

They embraced amidst the tall grasses, lips briefly pressed close in greeting.

'I hope you not be worrying for me,' she stated.

'It only matters that you be here now,' he replied with a smile as they slipped their arms about each other and walked to the concealment afforded by the aged tree.

'There was much whispering and little sleep thanks to what Seyeh had to tell,' she stated, quickly glancing over her shoulder.

'What be the matter?' he asked, seeing the haunted look upon her face.

'Nothing,' she said with a shake of her head.

Isaac brought them to a stop a couple of yards from the deep shadows that awaited their presence. 'There be something.' He searched her gaze.

'It be a feeling is all.'

'A feeling?'

'Like someone be watching,' she replied, looking down, abashed to admit the foolish disturbance. 'It set my skin a crawling and hastened my steps.'

He looked to the meadow's entrance, seeing nothing of note. 'If I be a gambling man I'd wager it were Seyeh's words done set it in you,' he stated as he turned back to her. 'Such things stir the soul and unsettle the mind.

There be many dreams tonight and not all be kindly recalled when dawn comes.'

Oneesha raised her head and looked into his kindly eyes, finding reason why she loved him in their warm depths. 'You stir my soul,' she whispered, leaning forward and kissing him.

They moved into the darkness beneath the willow and settled against the trunk, the bare backs of roots reaching out of the earth to either side. She cuddled into him, finding comfort and security in the closeness as his arm encircled her shoulders.

Isaac felt her hair upon his cheek as she rested her head upon his shoulder. All was still as they collected their thoughts and savoured their precious time together, its significance accentuated by its rarity.

Soft footfalls arose from the far side of the trunk.

They looked to the left, their eyes widened by uneasiness and neither daring to turn their heads. Oneesha's heart thundered, expecting to see Silas step into view as the sounds drew close.

A small doe stepped into view, oblivious to their presence. It moved into plain sight, sniffing the earth and then raising its head as if some sixth sense had alerted it to their presence.

The deer's nostrils flared as it sniffed the air. It looked out from beneath the boughs to the stillness of the meadow, ears rotating as it listened for potential threat.

They watched in enraptured silence. The trepidation fell from their expressions and Oneesha's pulse calmed as she quietly drew a long breath.

The doe flinched in sudden realisation of unexpected company, fur rippling with muscle tension. It took to the hoof, bounding out of the cover and through the grasses until it could no longer be seen in the starless darkness.

They sat staring after it for a while before Isaac turned.

'It be a sign,' he stated.

'A sign?'

'Change is a coming.'

She shifted her head upon his shoulder and looked up to his face. 'Venus say the same down by the river yesterday.'

'And she be right. I can feel it. It be hanging in the air like the scent of blossom before the fruiting.'

Oneesha smiled softly as she studied Isaac's shadowy features. He had a faraway expression on his face as he looked out to the meadow.

'You be thinking we should go,' she stated.

He felt her breath brush against his neck and turned to look down at her questioningly. 'Did you be saying something?'

Her smile grew. 'I said, you be thinking we should go.'

'Mayhap we should.'

She shook her head against his shoulder. 'We would not journey far before the hounds be catching us.'

'We could swim up the river,' he said. 'You be on my back,' he added as she opened her mouth to respond.

She averted her gaze. 'I would not take to the river,' she mumbled to his chest, a change of tone hinting at her feelings.

Isaac bowed his head and sought out her eyes, his own begging a question.

'I be feeling the spirits of the dead within its waters,' she said.

He studied her for a moment and then looked out towards the bull rushes to the left. 'I feel them too,' he admitted with a nod, 'but do not fear them.'

'I be not fearing them, but the whispering of the waters.'

They fell into silence for a few moments, the night offering no interruption.

'We could leave by another route,' suggested Isaac.

Oneesha lifted her head from him, hand resting upon his chest as she looked to his eyes. 'We stay,' she stated. 'We stay and pray the Lord sees fit to bring freedom for all our people.'

'If it be the Union that wins out.'

She nodded. 'What good be there in being whipped and beaten as a runaway when it may be freedom is coming?'

'It be coming,' he affirmed.

Isaac raised his head as the deer had some, nostrils flaring as he took a deep breath. 'Can you smell it blossoming?'

She smiled and nodded again. 'And I be one of the first to celebrate its fruiting when that day comes.'

He looked at her a moment and then rose to his feet, Oneesha moving back as he did so. 'Why be waiting?' he asked, bending and taking her hands, lifting her and then leading her out into the grasses.

She let out a short laugh of curious apprehension, unsure as to his meaning or motivation but his bright spontaneity a joy to behold.

Isaac brought them to a halt and turned to face her as he released her hands. 'May I be having this dance?' he asked, giving a little bow.

He linked the crook of his right arm in hers without waiting for a response. 'To freedom,' he said with a grin.

He began to dance, passing around Oneesha as she stood bemused, their bond turning her with him as she remained on the spot.

'What be you doing?' she said with a smile and shake of her head, another laugh escaping her lips.

'Celebrating freedom,' he stated, turning to link his other arm with hers and beginning to dance in the opposite direction. 'Dance with me.'

Feeling a little self-conscious, but wishing to release herself to the moment and infected by his enthusiasm, Oneesha began to dance with him. They skipped in circles, flattening the grasses. She laughed long and free, hair trailing down her shoulders and nightshirt fluttering in her wake.

The rain came without announcement, a deluge released from the heavens. It fell straight and turned the night grey with its presence, the meadow and its surroundings smeared and loosing definition.

They danced on, rainwater dripping down their happy faces, clothes clinging in cooling wetness.

Breathless and glistening, they eventually collapsed to the grasses side by side. Their chests heaved and their expressions were filled with contentment as the downpour continued unabated, their troubles rinsed away in the succulence of the night.

Oneesha took hold of his hand, entwining her fingers with his and clasping with the tightness of need. He turned his head to see it echoed in her dark eyes, which yearned for his closeness.

Isaac drew her to him, holding her in his arms as the humidity gave rise to a thin mist which hung over the meadow, the rain pattering on the grasses about them.

'My heart be yours, Isaac,' she said into his ear as she lay draped over him, the whisper giving him chills.

'And mine be yours,' he replied, looking to the sky and praying their liberty would come soon.

Oneesha closed her eyes, her senses filled with his presence and wishing she did not have to endure the vacancy of parting when they arrived back at the slave quarters. She longed to lay with him through the hours of darkness and wake to find him beside her.

Raising her head, she moved her lips to his. They kissed with an aching tenderness only known in stolen moments. Her hands went to his wet face, cupping its strong contours with a soft touch. She felt his heartbeat against her as she lay over him, running a finger along his

73

lips when the caress came to an end, taking in his features as she looked upon him with hooded eyes.

'It be time to be going back,' said Isaac with regret, brushing hair back from her face.

Oneesha nodded, bending to kiss him once more, holding his gaze.

They sat up, the rain steady. Mist surrounded them, a still and ghostly blanket gathering over the landscape.

'It be like cotton,' commented Oneesha sadly as she stood, the reality of their lives rising like the dust of their toils, sullying her mind after the respite of the fleeting happiness they'd shared.

Isaac took her hand without responding. She turned to him and sighed.

'I could not live without you,' she stated, 'without us.'

His brow creased as he regarded her.

Oneesha looked down at her feet. 'That be why I not be holding with running to the north,' she admitted. 'If we was caught and they…' She took a breath. '…They took you from me.' She raised her head and held his gaze meaningfully.

Isaac ached when he saw the tumult in her eyes. 'There be no one going to take me from you.' He took hold of her other hand and moved to stand before her. 'We be staying and freedom will find us in time.'

'No more talk of running?'

'No more talk of running,' he confirmed, tightening his grip on her hands in reassurance.

Oneesha managed to raise a faint smile. He reached forward and softly stroked the dampness of her cheek.

They set off, the mist stirring in their wake. The rain thinned as they passed into the cotton fields, Isaac leading the way.

The upper floor of the Big House came into view above the persimmon grove and they paused when they saw diffused light spilling from the window on the far right. Taking a wider route than usual, they moved between the rows of dripping plants, soil becoming caked upon their bare feet.

Reaching the far corner of the gently sloping north field, they looked to the buildings on the other side of the track that passed to the east. A lantern's meagre light shone through the mist and rain as it passed alongside the bunkhouse beyond the cotton store, the vague shape of a farmhand visible as it hung from the barrel of his shotgun.

Isaac glanced back as they crouched by the three-bar fence, finding Oneesha looking at him with concern.

'I never done seen anyone patrolling before,' she commented in a whisper.

He thought for a moment. 'Mayhap Master Canyon worries we be hearing about the Union and be making sure no one takes to their feet,' he replied.

'What if someone be running?'

Isaac shook his head. 'There be no baying. If someone had run the hounds would be loosed on their heels.'

Oneesha nodded to herself as she looked to the hazy lantern, a halo of yellow light cast about it. Isaac turned back to the buildings, seeing no sign of other lanterns as the solitary farmhand passed around the end of the building and was hidden from sight by the cotton store. A stain of faint light in the misted darkness marked his progress, fading and then vanishing altogether.

'Quickly,' he said over his shoulder, rising and taking them across the track.

They passed along the cotton store and hurried to the bunkhouse wall.

His back to the slats, Isaac moved forward and peered around into the yard that rested between them and their destination. The farmhand was near the far end, his silhouette obscuring the lantern light.

'Make haste to your cabin and don't be waiting for me,' he whispered. 'Go!'

Oneesha scampered from the concealment. The sound of the rain hid her hasty steps and the paleness of her nightshirt was masked by the mist as she made her way across the open ground.

Isaac watched with pulse racing, glancing at the patrolling figure, who continued to walk away unawares. When he looked back across the yard he found that she'd vanished from sight and took a breath of relief.

He moved out from the rear of the bunkhouse, feet squelching in the mud as he ran towards the cabins, body tremulous with adrenalin. His shoulders were tight as he concentrated his gaze ahead and prayed there would be no shout of discovery.

Isaac reached the rear of the women's cabin with his heart pounding. Hurrying to the far corner, he then sprinted between the two slave dormitories, passing the benches resting there.

Arriving at the door to the men's quarters, he took hold of the handle and glanced over his shoulder. The farmhand was turning his way and he quickly slipped into the building, the sharp creak of hinges making him wince.

His damp and muddied footsteps marking his passage, Isaac went to his cot on the far side of the room and took up his bed cover. He hastened back to the door, dropping to his hands and knees. Desperately rubbing at the floorboards, he listened for any sign of approach over the drumming of the rain as he shuffled backwards.

Slow steps drew out of the night as Isaac's back bumped into his bed. He looked to the floor, the darkness offering no hint as to his success in hiding his tracks. Climbing onto the cot, he pulled the cover over him to conceal his sodden clothes.

The sound of the door opening was followed by heavy steps upon the boards. A golden glow illuminated the interior as he lay still and stared at the wall, the shadow of his body cast upon it.

The farmhand remained by the door. He raised the lantern higher and Isaac's silhouette moved down the slats as if slipping into the crack between them and the cot as his ears were filled with the rush of blood.

There was a tortuous pause and Isaac prayed that no sign of his passage remained.

The farmhand turned and left the cabin, darkness rushing in as the door closed. The fall of his boots passed along the side of the building as Isaac let out his breath and his body sagged with the release of tension.

'The liberty afforded us.'

The mocking whisper drifted to him and he knew without turning that it was Anthony who had spoken. Ignoring the comment, he tried to push the discomfort of his wet clothing from his mind and hoped sleep would soon come. He was in need of recuperation in readiness for another day of labour in the west field.

Shifting, he closed his eyes to the pitch. His mind drifted, thoughts turning to Oneesha, as they often did. He saw her joy as she danced with him in the meadow, her unfettered laughter swelling his heart.

Isaac took a breath, a profound feeling of loneliness coming upon him as he listened to the rain upon the roof and wished for the release of slumber.

13

Oneesha bent and reached under the cot with the switches of the broom as she cleaned the women's sleeping quarters, the door wide and dappled sunlight resting on the floorboards after passing through the tall trees on the far side of the men's cabin. A pair of doves cooed in the branches as moisture lifted from the roofs in tendrils of steam, the morning yet young as the heat grew.

She recalled the previous night's meeting with a shake of her head, hair tightly bound in a blue cloth. 'Mayhap it were but a dream,' she muttered to herself as she hurried the dirt up the aisle with the tough bristles, her help required in the kitchens once she'd finished cleaning.

As she moved towards the door she heard the approach of measured footsteps. She stiffened, knowing that it was one of the farmhands approaching from the sound of their boots upon the earth, the slaves of the plantation barefooted.

A shadow fell across the boards before her, the golden shards of dust that swirled in the air swallowed by its darkness.

'Ain't this a happy coincidence?'

Oneesha's chest tightened at the sound of Silas' voice. She didn't respond, but continued with the brushing, bending and passing the switches beneath the last of the cots by the door.

'I asked you a question, nigger.'

'Yessir,' she replied, giving a curt nod.

'Ain't you got a "good day" for me?' There was amusement in his tone.

She paused. 'Good day,' she said without looking at him, the tone of her words more a farewell than a greeting.

Oneesha began to brush the pile of dirt towards the door. He put his left foot in the way, his snakeskin boot crunching on the detritus.

'Let me see them pretty brown eyes of yours.'

She raised her face to find him grinning at her. He reached forward to brush her cheek and she flinched.

His eyes tightened. The slap came quick and hard, its sharp sound filling the interior of the cabin. She recoiled, taking a step back, cheek stinging and eyes watering.

'Now you be listening to me, nigger,' he hissed as he took a step inside. 'I'm gonna do what I want with you and you ain't gonna struggle unless you want a beating and time in the hole.'

Her throat constricted and she swallowed hard. Movement caught her eye over his shoulder and she saw the figure of her shrouded Mistress pass by.

'Mistress Canyon!' she exclaimed.

Silas turned to look back, catching sight of the dark figure passing beyond sight around the end of the men's dormitory.

Oneesha took her chance, rushing past him and out of the door.

He turned and attempted to grab her, catching the sleeve of her faded blue dress before she stepped out of his reach. The handkerchief she kept tucked there as a memento of the times spent with Isaac beneath the willow was loosed and tumbled to the ground.

Silas crouched and plucked it up as she watched. He straightened as he lifted and studied it.

'Such a pretty thing to be belonging to a slave,' he stated, turning his gaze to her. 'You steal it from the big house?'

She shook her head. 'It be a gift,' she replied nervously, fearful of punishment despite her words being the truth.

He studied her a moment as he considered whether she was lying. 'I think I'll be a keeping it until next time we meet.' His lop-sided grin returned.

Oneesha stared helplessly as he tucked the pale cloth into a pocket on his britches. Turning, she hurried away, following in the direction that she'd seen Mistress Canyon take.

'I'll be seeing you soon,' called Silas behind her, his words containing a promise that gave her chills and raised the hairs upon her forearms.

Walking around the end of the cabin, she spied Mistress Canyon amidst the Spanish moss hanging from the wide branches on the far side of the north track. She was seated on the swing that Miss Lilly had once used, motionless and bowed as the feathers of moss swayed in the slight breeze.

Oneesha's steps faltered, finding no reason to approach the woman. Glancing over her shoulder, she found no evidence of Silas despite expecting him to be watching.

Veering to the right, she moved to the rear of the slave quarters, making haste along the back of the men's cabin, she paused when she reached the corner and looked between the two dormitories. The door to the women's was still wide, but the farmhand had apparently departed.

She briefly pondered closing the entrance, but decided against it when the image of Silas lurking within came to mind. Instead, she crossed the few yards between the buildings and made her way along the back of the second cabin.

With a glance around the side, she hurried beyond the scattering of sheds and made her way to the rear of the Big House, longing for the relative safety of the kitchens and Seyeh's welcome company. She swept into the house, passing along a short corridor as she thought about her Mistress, feeling a pang of sympathy. Ascending a small set of steps, she entered the kitchens through the door at the top.

Seyeh turned from the table at the centre, a chopping board before her where the carcass of a chicken rested, knife stilled in her hand. Mitilde stood opposite her, hands white with flour and as she mixed Cajun batter in a large earthenware bowl.

'I be expecting you earlier,' said the older woman, the tone of her voice stern and her expression showing her state of agitation. 'We have much to do in preparation.

The funeral be not long from now and there will be twenty people seeking to be fed at the wake.'

'My pardon, Seyeh,' she apologised as she took an apron down from a hook, putting it on and tying it about her waist, Seyeh returning her attention to cutting the feet off the fowl in preparation for cooking. 'Where be the others?'

'Venus and Rose be preparing the dining room, Angie be sweeping the front porch and Casius be seeing to Master Canyon,' she replied as she cut just beneath the knuckle of bone, removing the lower portion of one of the chicken's legs.

'If Silas done had his way I would have been delayed further,' she revealed, the older woman immediately looking up at her.

'He tried to take you?' asked Seyeh, Mitilde falling still and turning to Oneesha.

'That were his intention, but I be lucky this time.'

'The vegetables,' said Seyeh, nodding at a pair of burlap sacks resting near the door through which Oneesha had arrived and studying her a moment. 'He hit you,' she stated, noting the redness of her cheek.

Oneesha nodded. 'If Mistress Canyon not be passing it would have been much worse,' she responded. 'She be sitting lonesome on Miss Lilly's swing and I thought to take her out some honeyed water, like she likes it. The heat be pressing after the rains last night and her all in black too.'

Seyeh's expression softened and a thin smile dawned as she regarded her. 'You have a kind heart, Neesh.'

Oneesha glanced at her as she opened the first of the sacks.

'I s'ppose I can spare you a little longer,' said the older woman, her smile broadening.

'You be sure?' she asked in surprise.

Seyeh nodded. 'But hurry and get it done.'

The two women at the table continued with their preparations as Oneesha took a glass from a cabinet and filled it from a pail. Seeking out a jar of honey, she set it on the counter that ran the length of the wall and dipped in a teaspoon, taking up some of the golden contents and turning them to reel in the thick strand still drawing down. Stirring the honey into the water with vigorous motion, she lifted the glass to see most had dissolved, the water a little discoloured as the remainder turned in decreasing motion to settle at the bottom and she licked the last from the spoon.

She hastened from the room, exiting the way she'd entered. Narrowing her eyes against the brightness, she stepped from the Big House and made her way left, passing the collection of plantation buildings while keeping a keen eye for any sign of Silas, gladly finding him nowhere in sight.

Rounding the back of the men's cabin, she set eyes on Mistress Canyon. She was still seated on the swing as the moss hanging from the wide branches shivered about her.

Oneesha slowed her pace as she approached, feeling apprehensive and wondering as to the wisdom of her actions, thinking that the grieving woman may find her interruption both unwarranted and unwanted. She passed beneath the outer-reaches of the boughs, ducking past trails of moss and coming to a standstill five yards from the dark figure.

'Mistress Canyon,' she said with a nervous curtsey. 'I done and brought you some honeyed water.' She held up the glass.

Her Mistress didn't respond and she shifted with growing discomfort.

'I be leaving it here for you,' she stated, tentatively stepping forward and placing the glass on the grass beside the swing.

Taking a couple of steps back, she gave another curtsey and turned.

'Can you hear the river whispering?' The question was faint.

She turned to her Mistress, chill fingers passing up her spine.

Mistress Canyon slowly raised her head. 'I hear it,' she stated, 'it calls to me day and night.' Her words were weak and filled with a sense of bleak inevitability.

'It whispers from my daughter, its scent marking the claim it has upon her soul.'

Oneesha looked to the veil, seeing pale skin beyond its lace. Her gaze settled on her Mistress' eyes, finding them surrounded by the shadows of sleepless nights and raw with loss. They spoke of a broken woman sitting upon the swing, wishing to be renewed to the carefree innocence that had once abided there.

She tried to think of a suitable response, glancing to the cotton fields beyond the trees and briefly thinking of Isaac in the west field. Unable to find the right words, she simply curtseyed once again.

'I be needed in the kitchens and will take my leave, with your pardon.'

Mistress Canyon nodded vaguely.

Oneesha hesitated and then turned. She walked away with a measured pace that quickened once she was hidden from the woman's sight, wishing to be away and find the warmth of Seyeh's company.

14

The blade sliced into the broken soil and Isaac shovelled it away. He was dripping with sweat in the noonday sun as Anthony lifted the felling axe and brought it down on roots which had already been uncovered.

He turned to Wilson, the farmhand seated on one of the piles of lumber, as he had been the previous day. His hat was covering his eyes as he reclined, his shotgun leaning beside him.

Isaac's gaze moved to the pail and parcel of food that Angie had carried to the field, lingering briefly before returning to the Big House in order to get ready for Miss Lilly's wake. He licked his cracked lips as his scalp itched, the dampness of the rainfall during the night long since evaporated and dust rising with every labour to coat and irritate his skin.

'Be it time to break now, Boss?' he asked.

Wilson didn't stir.

'Boss?' he called with greater volume as he saw a fly settle on the farmhand's bulbous nose. There was no reaction to its presence and Isaac's brow creased.

'Something be wrong,' he stated, turning to Anthony as the axe fell again.

The other slave let the head rest buried in the root and turned to Wilson. 'He be sleeping, is all.'

Isaac shook his head. 'There be more than that.'

He leant forward and rested his shovel against the stump. Walking the ten yards to the lumber pile, he came to a halt a short distance before the farmhand.

'Boss?' he said again, watching the fly moving upon Wilson's nose, another upon his cheek.

There was still no reaction.

Isaac stepped up to him as Anthony walked over. He tentatively reached out and took hold of the brim of Wilson's hat, the fly taking to the air as he lifted it a little and bent to look at his eyes. They remained closed and there was no movement beneath the lids.

'Be he dead?' asked Anthony.

Isaac let the brim settle back on the bridge of Wilson's nose. He cupped his left hand and held it before the farmhand's nostrils before shaking his head. 'He be breathing,' he stated. 'Mayhap he done got himself a case of the wilt,' he added, turning to Anthony, finding the other slave's gaze resting on the shotgun.

'We be doing nothing stupid,' he said.

Anthony looked to him unkindly. 'What we be calling stupid be different things.'

'We should take him to the bunkhouse and be telling Silas,' he suggested, ignoring the remark.

'You want we should carry him?'

Isaac nodded. 'There be no horse so that be the only way,' he replied, Wilson having walked with them to the field after rising without time or will to saddle a mount.

'You be carrying him. I won't lift a finger to help one of the white folk unless I be told to do so.'

'Well, I be telling you,' responded Isaac with anger, turning to Anthony.

They stared at each other for a while as they stood in the blazing sunlight, a battle of wills occurring in the silence between them.

'I be needing a drink first.' Anthony turned away and walked to where the pail rested by the wall.

Crouching as Isaac watched, he raised the ladle and drank deep before refilling it and pouring its contents over his head, relishing its cool touch down the back of his neck and a tremor rising to his shoulders. Taking another drink, he rose and returned at a purposefully slow pace.

'You be a good slave,' he offered as an insult, moving to put his arm around Wilson's shoulders and lifting him.

Isaac stared at him a moment longer and then moved to the farmhand's left, the two slaves supporting his weight. He glanced back at the shotgun, deciding to leave it where it leant against the lumber, thinking it unwise for either of them to carry the weapon to the plantation buildings.

They began towards the gateway, Wilson's hat slipping and falling to the dust as his head hung loose. Isaac glanced at it as the farmhand's legs trailed behind, boots leaving shallow furrows in their wake.

They passed out of the field and moved along the track between the cotton fields, slaves working along the avenues of plants pausing to look curiously over. A mounted farmhand on the left spied their passage, rifle butt resting on his thigh and barrel pointed to the sky as he shaded his eyes with his free hand.

With a nudge of his heels, he moved along the row. Reaching the end, the mount was encouraged into a canter as it passed along the edge of the field, Isaac and Anthony watching as the farmhand joined the track and came towards them. He brought the horse to a halt ten yards ahead, its right flank turned to them so as to bar the way.

'And what in the good Lord's name do you think you're doing?' asked Rusty, holding his rifle at the ready, cropped beard accentuating his angular jaw.

'He be struck down with the wilt and we be taking him to the bunkhouse,' replied Isaac, glancing over his shoulder as another farmhand rode up behind them.

Rusty regarded them for a moment. 'What you niggers done with his gun?'

'It be back in the west field, Boss.'

He looked over at the other farmhand and gave a nod in answer to a silent question. The sound of the horse behind them moving off soon followed, a cloud of dust drifting along the track on the light breeze and briefly shrouding them.

'Well, don't just stand there,' stated Rusty, pulling his horse to the side of the track and waving them by.

They began to walk by with Wilson's unconscious form between them.

'You could be putting him on your horse,' mumbled Anthony.

'What you say, nigger?' Rusty scowled down at the slave.

'I be saying nothing, Boss,' he responded without looking over, adjusting his hold around Wilson's shoulders.

'You better not be giving me sass, boy,' said Rusty as he took up the reins and nudged the horse into an easy walk beside them. 'Unless you're looking to spend some time in the hole.'

Anthony remained silent.

They moved along the track in silence. Isaac wiped sweat from his brow with the back of his arm, eyes stinging.

Reaching the edge of the field, Rusty pulled his mount to a halt as they continued, the Big House and collection of buildings on its western side coming into view through the small grove of trees to the right. Isaac and Anthony moved through the dappled shade and joined the track that went south, passing the cotton store and walking alongside the slave quarters.

Isaac's gaze was drawn by the sight of Oneesha at the well beside the three-bar fence that marked the front boundary of the Big House grounds. She sat on the edge of the low wall and drew up a pail through the gap beside her, one half of the well's circular wooden cap removed and resting atop the other. Seyeh was standing just beyond, two pails by her feet as she waited.

Silas came into view, moving towards Oneesha from the bunkhouse to the left. There was a grin on his face and Isaac's pulse increased in response.

She gripped the rope tightly as she hauled the pail from the shadows, struggling as she brought it out and over the rim and unaware of the farmhand's approach.

'Let me help you with that,' said Silas, his arms passing around her and breath wafting against the back of her neck.

She jolted her shoulders in surprised response, catching him in the chest, Isaac stiffening as he watched. Silas spun her round and struck her across the cheek with the back of his hand.

Isaac was about to release his hold on Wilson in order to go to her aid when Anthony suddenly let go. He sprinted towards the tussle as the farmhand grasped Oneesha firmly by the shoulders.

'Leave her be,' stated Seyeh, stepping forward.

Silas heard Anthony approach from behind. He jabbed his elbow back just as the slave reached him, catching Anthony on the chin and sending him sprawling in the dust.

The farmhand rounded on him, drawing his gun as Oneesha ran to Seyeh, the older woman taking her into her arms.

'You wanna try that again, nigger?' growled Silas, the pistol steady and aimed at the slave's chest.

Anthony glared at him from the ground.

'I ain't heard no reply.'

'No, Sir,' he replied, the second word spoken with distaste.

Two more farmhands hurriedly approached from the bunkhouse, rifles held at the ready. They came to a stop a few yards from the prone slave and pointed their weapons at him. Anthony raised his hands, elbows resting in the dirt.

'Two days in the hole,' stated Silas without taking his hot gaze from the slave.

'Take up a pail. We come back for more later,' Seyeh instructed Oneesha with soft urgency, wishing to be away before Silas had the chance to return his attention to the girl.

They each took up a bucket and began to make their way to the Big House, the older woman putting her arm about Oneesha comfortingly as Isaac watched them leave. He was kept in place by the farmhand slumped against his side, though he ached to go to her side, the sight of Silas striking her having knotted his stomach with frustrated angst.

The men who had walked over took hold of Anthony's arms with their free hands and began to drag him away. He put up no struggle as they took him to the hole, which was located in a patch of barren earth on the far side of the cotton store where it was said no plant would grow.

Silas turned to Isaac, gun still drawn and held at his side. 'What the hell are you looking at, nigger?'

Isaac averted his gaze. 'Nothing, Boss.'

He heard the sound of the farmhand's approach over the disturbance of Anthony being taken along the track behind him. Silas' snakeskin boots drew into his field of vision as he came to stop a few yards before him.

'You got something you want to say to me?'

Isaac shook his head.

Silas regarded him for a few moments before holstering the pistol. 'Where are you planning on taking old White Cake here?' he asked, using the nickname with which the farmhand had been dubbed due to his fondness for desserts and consequently bulging stomach.

'We be taking him to the bunkhouse,' replied Isaac. 'He got the wilt.'

'Be that so?' Silas looked at Wilson's thinning brown hair, a bald patch apparent at the crown. He took hold at the fringe and lifted the farmhand's head, staring at his face, seeing the flush upon his wide cheeks.

'It seems that you be right, nigger,' he stated, letting Wilson's head loll forward once again.

A film of grease was left upon his palm and he made a show of being disgusted by its presence, wiping his hand on Isaac's shirt before turning to the bunkhouse. 'Pete,' he called, seeing the man exit, 'come on over here and take White Cake inside.'

Pete walked over without enthusiasm, taking Wilson's limp form and struggling to take him back to the building. Silas and Isaac remained standing opposite other, a short silence lingering between them.

'Why you still standing there, nigger?' asked the farmhand incredulously.

'What you want I should do, Boss?' replied Isaac, his head remaining bowed.

'Getting back to work would be the first thing. Now get your black ass back over to the west field. Them stumps ain't going to pop out the ground all by themselves.'

'But there be no one to watch over me.'

'The good Lord will have to be enough. There ain't no one to spare for one lone nigger.'

'Yessir,' nodded Isaac.

Silas cupped Isaac's chin and raised his head. 'Now don't go doing anything dumb like running off, your hear.'

'No, Sir.'

'Them dogs sure do like a bit of nigger meat.'

'Yessir.'

'Now get on over to the west field and get to work, boy.' Silas released his chin with a flick of his wrist, Isaac's head snapping to the side.

'Yessir,' he replied, taking a step back before turning.

Isaac set off, feeling Silas' gaze resting on his back and its weight adding haste to his steps. His thoughts turned to Oneesha and he longed to see her, hoping they would meet by chance when evening came and finding solace in the knowledge that she was in Seyeh's care.

15

Isaac hacked at the thick root with the felling axe. The sun hung low, its evening warmth on his face. Arms aching and covered in a thick layer of sweat-smeared dust, he raised the axe once again, swinging it down to the chop of the blade biting into the wood.

Pausing, he rubbed his left eye with the top of his arm, leaning his head into it and then blinking to clear his vision. He hefted the axe and was about to bring it down when the sensation of being watched came upon him.

Isaac went still and turned to look over his shoulder. Standing in the gateway was Oneesha, a smile upon her face.

Letting the axe drop to the dust, he went to her. Walking quickly over, he took her into his arms, holding her tight and close.

'You be a sight for sore eyes,' he said, looking to her face and gaze moving to her cheek, seeing it brushed with the red of swelling.

'I be fine,' she said, seeing his expression tighten and taking hold of his hand.

'Can you stay?' he asked.

Oneesha looked back and then led him to the wall, seating herself against the stone beside the lumber piles and drawing Isaac down beside her. 'I done brought you something,' she said with a sparkle in her eyes, reaching into the pocket at the front of her dress.

She withdrew a pale serviette and passed it to him. He rested it upon his lap as he sat cross-legged, Oneesha watching him unwrap what was concealed within, an expectant smile upon her face. Pulling back the folds, Isaac found a few strips of Cajun chicken, the aroma of their spices rising to him and his expression brightening.

'They be left over from the wake. Seyeh say it be fine to bring them to you when my duties be finished,' she explained as he lowered his head and wafted the smell with his hand, taking a deep breath and then sighing it out, mouth watering.

'And for when you be done with them,' she said, withdrawing another serviette parcel from the pocket and holding it out to him.

Isaac looked at it in pleasant surprise, eyes moving to hers. 'You be spoiling me.'

'You deserve it,' she grinned.

He took the second parcel and placed it beside the first before opening it to reveal three sweetened oat cakes. He chuckled to himself and shook his head before turning back to her.

'My thanks, Neesh,' he said, leaning to her and giving her a kiss. 'It be a king's feast.'

Isaac took up a strip of chicken, offering it to her. She shook her head and he took a small bite, savouring the taste and leaning back against the warm stones.

'How were the wake?' he asked, putting the rest of the piece into his mouth.

'Mistress Canyon done go straight to her rooms when they returned from the burial and Rose took up a tray. I just be glad to be out of those clothes,' she said, Isaac well aware that she disliked the maid's uniform she had to wear when called upon to serve in the Big House, its starched stiffness and restriction making her feel uncomfortable.

He nodded as he ate another piece of chicken, a feeling of peacefulness coming upon him in the evening hush. 'A free life must feel this way,' he reflected with an easy smile.

Oneesha looked at his profile and then rested her head upon his shoulder. 'It feels good,' she said softly, laying a hand on his knee and breathing in his raw scent.

They sat together in brief contentment, looking out over the stumps and bare earth. Small swarms of mosquitoes were gathered in places, rising and falling with the faint breeze. Rays of gold slanted through the trees opposite, the sun's blaze becoming a glitter as its heated ferocity was subdued in slow demise

Isaac folded the empty serviette as he finished off the chicken. Taking up one of the oat cakes, he broke it in half, moist crumbs falling to his lap. Passing a piece to Oneesha, she took it silently and they both partook of the tender sweetness that had been scented with rose petals.

Finishing, Isaac took up one of the cakes that remained and gave it to her. Picking up the other, he raised it to his lips and his hand stilled as he looked across the field thoughtfully.

'It should have been me,' he stated softly.

'What you say?' she asked, turning to look up at his face.

Isaac looked down at her honeyed features and stroked her cheek affectionately. 'It should have been me that be running to help you at the well.'

Oneesha held his gaze firmly and shook her head. 'Then it be you down the hole and we not be sitting here.'

He pondered and then kissed her again. 'That be true.'

They fell into a brief silence again.

'The investigator done come when was finishing up.'

'Investigator?' asked Isaac, placing his arm about her shoulders and drawing her closer.

'He be hired by Master Canyon to investigate the killing of Miss Lilly,' she responded, head to his chest and arm across him.

'Be he staying in the Big House?'

Oneesha nodded. 'He done told Rose not to disturb him. He say he not want to see anyone but Master Canyon till morning.'

Isaac thought back to the start of the week when he'd been unable to locate Anthony's whereabouts. Despite his suspicions, he wouldn't say a word to the investigator for fear a hanging would be the result, evidence or no evidence. He couldn't say for sure where Anthony was and if anything had been found to link him to the murder there would already be a noose about his neck.

'What you be thinking about?' asked Oneesha.

'Nothing worth saying,' he replied, looking down at her regretfully. 'You should go back before you be missed.'

'I thought you be coming with me,' she said with obvious disappointment.

Isaac looked across the field at the trees, the sun still shining through the boughs. 'There be another hours work as yet.'

'But there be nobody watching over you.'

'They sure to see me if I go back,' he responded.

Oneesha frowned and sighed. Feeling her reluctance to leave him and not wishing her to find punishment her reward for lingering, he gently moved her aside and got to his feet after folding the serviettes.

He held them out to her with a regretful smile. 'You best be getting back,' he said as she stood and took them from him. 'My thanks for the food and the company.'

'Mayhap we see each other when you be back?' she asked hopefully.

'Mayhap we will,' he replied.

Isaac leant forward and they kissed in parting. Oneesha turned and walked to the gateway, glancing back at him and raising her hand before moving onto the track. He watched for a while, the dusk gathering about her as she trod softly through the blue shadows.

Turning, he made his way back to the stump where he'd been working. Isaac took up the axe, feeling his muscles complain, and began to swing it once more.

16

He woke to the gloom of dawn's early light. He opened his eyes to the cabin wall, waiting for them to adjust to the meagre illumination gaining entry between the slats of the shutters covering the small windows.

His thoughts turned to Oneesha. He imagined her asleep in the women's dormitory, her lids fluttering as she dreamt. He'd never witnessed her sleeping and wondered at the beauty of her restful countenance, envisaging himself brushing her cheek and stroking her hair as she lay beside him.

Able to see well enough for the task he intended to perform, he rolled over, scanning the other cots about the room for any signs of wakefulness. There were none.

Slipping his hand beneath the straw-filled pillow, he retrieved a piece of sackcloth that he'd stowed there and then sought out the thin length of burnt wood that had been hidden alongside it, taking a few moments to locate it. He leant on his left shoulder, the cloth resting on his palm as he held it before his face and began to create a simple sketch.

The scrape of the wood moving across the fibres was punctuated by the rise and fall of snoring. Hearing movement from one of the nearby cots, Isaac paused momentarily, Oscar groaning as he turned and then settled back into slumber.

The picture was soon completed and he looked at it with a thin smile of satisfaction. Later, he'd collect the figures that were resting against the wall of the west field and hoped he would find the chance to place them upon Oneesha's pillow.

The approach of booted steps caused him to quickly tuck the cloth and wood back into their concealment. He lowered his head to the pillow and closed his eyes just as the door opened at the far side of the cabin.

'Rise and shine,' called Silas, banging his fist on the wall. 'Time for you no good niggers to get up and get to work.'

The interior was filled with disturbance, cots creaking as the men arose, legs swinging over the sides and bare feet upon the floor boards.

Isaac pulled back the bed cover and got up, standing and stretching, pain in his lower back causing him to wince and his shoulders stiff. He joined the others as they began to file out of the door, Silas stepping to the side and staring at them as they exited.

'I ain't never seen such a sorry bunch of niggers in my life,' he commented with a shake of his head.

They lined up as Seyeh doled out bowls of thin soup with crusts of bread, a large cooking pot resting on the rearmost bench. Those who had been served sat down, raising the bland offering and supping without enthusiasm as the sun peered over the eastern horizon and bathed the space between the two cabins in its light.

'Cesar,' called Silas.

'Yessir,' replied the aged slave.

'You and Ben are cleaning out the shed behind the cotton Store. Oscar, you're with Isaac in the west field. White Cake ain't in a fit state to oversee, so you'll have Pete for company. The rest of you be getting on with what you were doing yesterday.'

Isaac nodded his thanks to Seyeh as she filled his bowl and handed him a piece of bread. He turned to find no room at the other benches and so seated himself near the cooking pot.

Lifting the bowl to his lips, he felt the gentle warmth on his face before sipping the watery offering, finding little by way of taste. Biting off a mouthful of bread, he chewed on its staleness, yawning and blinking away tears from his eyes as he felt the sunlight on his cheeks that announced another day of toil.

17

Oneesha knelt before a wash tub on the back lawn, her knees dampened by the last of the night's moisture. The sun had risen over the house and the grass glittered about her as she cleaned the linens used for the wake, using the gentle rub of her thumbs to shift the stains when possible, the abrasion of the scrubbing board too severe for the laced edging.

She dipped the tablecloth she was holding beneath the suds, a thoughtful look upon her face. Her desire to see Isaac again the previous evening had not been fulfilled and she wondered if they'd find each other's company that day, though many were the times when she saw no sight of him.

She rubbed at a yellow stain that was proving stubborn and wished she had company with which to pass the time. When she washed the farmhand's clothes the following day she'd have Seyeh and at least one of the other women beside her, and for that she was grateful.

A sudden chill ran through her. The back of her neck tingled and Oneesha had the distinct feeling she was not alone.

Glancing over her shoulder, she expected to find Silas approaching, but found no one in sight. The sensation persisted and she shifted nervously, feeling unsettled as she turned her attention back to the task, lifting the cloth and wringing it out with a practiced twist.

She glanced over her shoulder in alarm as a clatter arose from the direction of the cotton store. Eyes narrowing, she scanned the buildings beyond the trees where the washing lines hung, looking for the source of the disturbance.

A moment passed and then she spied Ben exiting the small shed at the back of the store, a wooden box in his hands and Cesar following behind with an armful of rusting tools. She watched them curiously as they moved away and out of sight, obscured from view by other stores and the bunkhouse.

Oneesha stared after them for a while as she pondered their activity. Shaking her head, she cleared her thoughts and inspected the cloth, holding it up and letting it partially unravel.

She tensed in momentary fright. Her gaze had been drawn beyond the tablecloth to the dark figure standing in a high window of the Big House. Though she couldn't see Mistress Canyon's face behind the veil, Oneesha felt sure that she was watching and another shiver ran through her.

Her hands trembling slightly as a result of the shock, she lowered the cloth and her gaze, taking a steadying breath. Sinking it into the waters, she watched as bubbles escaped its edges to join with the suds, glittering with sunlight before softly bursting, their demise a small sound on the edge of her hearing as her senses prickled.

She tried to concentrate, to push the presence of her Mistress from her mind, but it lingered there, its shadow echoing that of the black-clad woman in the window.

'Can you hear the river whispering?'

The question sighed through the corridors of her memory like a breath of wind.

Oneesha looked up. The window was vacant, Mistress Canyon having retreated into the gloom beyond the pane.

Swallowing and feeling distinctly uneasy, she turned to the tub once again. A flare of colour to her left caught her eye and she found a butterfly perched on the edge of the basket resting beside her as it bathed in the warmth.

She watched as it flexed its dusted wings, wondering if it could be the same one she'd discovered in the cabin. A gentle smile graced her lips as she imagined it was giving thanks for the liberty she had afforded it.

She was about to reach out her hand when it took to the wing. It flittered above the tub, attracted by the scent of lilacs. Circling, it then flew off over the lawn towards the persimmon grove on the far side of the Big House.

Oneesha watched it dwindle, smile fading as it vanished from sight. She sighed and returned to her work, wiping her brow with a forearm and hands once more entering the water to take up the tablecloth.

18

Isaac's attention was taken by the quick beat of hoofs as he and Oscar secured a rope around the tree stump in readiness for it to be torn from the ground with the help of the workhorse they'd brought to the west field. Silas was approaching at a gallop, Pete moving to the gateway with his rifle cradled again his chest.

'It's time,' announced Silas as he drew his mount to a stop, the creature snorting and bucking its head as a pall of dust hung in the air about it.

Pete nodded. 'I'll bring 'em straight over.'

Silas looked to the slaves and grinned before turning and setting off again at a steady pace. Oscar glanced over the stump questioningly and Isaac shrugged, both uncertain as to the meaning of Silas' brief visit.

'Right you two, drop what you're doing and follow me,' said Pete as he turned and wondered over to his horse.

'Where we be going, Boss?' asked Oscar as they both hesitated with the rope in their hands.

'You'll find out soon enough,' replied the farmhand over his shoulder, taking holding of the pommel and mounting after sliding the rifle into the holster resting against the horse's flank.

Isaac and Oscar exchanged glances again and then released the rope. They moved towards the entrance of the field as Pete rode over and waited.

Isaac quickly went to the wall beside the entrance, picking up the figures he'd made and tucking them into the back of his britches.

'What you doing there, nigger?'

'I just be getting a drink of water, Boss,' he replied, making a show of taking up the ladle, holding it up to Pete before drinking from it.

'I ain't heard no permission being asked.'

'Sorry, Boss,' he responded, hurrying over as he wiped his lips.

Pete stared down at him unkindly. 'You boys keep up or there'll be no supper tonight,' he stated, whipping the reins and giving a kick with his heels.

The horse set off at a canter, Isaac and Oscar setting off to run in the dust rising behind. They made their way between the cotton fields, watched by those working between the rows. The plantation buildings soon came into sight, Isaac wiping his eyes as perspiration dripped into them, his scalp itching with the irritation of grime.

Joining the north-south track, they followed it to the slave quarters, Pete pulling up at the far end of the two cabins. They stumbled up behind, muscles straining, mouths thick with phlegm.

The farmhand dismounted and looked them up and down. 'You.' He pointed at Isaac.

'Yessir,' he panted in response.

'Wait in the cabin. Oscar, you come with me.'

Oscar looked to Isaac, concern in his gaze.

'Get a hurry on, nigger,' scolded Pete over his shoulder as he began to walk away between the cabins.

Isaac watched at Oscar nervously followed after the farmhand, still catching his breath, legs aching and weary. The young slave glanced back before rounding the far end of the women's dormitory and walking out of sight, his eyes filled with fear.

Taking a few more deep breaths, Isaac looked around, checking that no one was watching him. Seeing that he was unobserved, he went with haste to the door of the men's cabin. Striding to his cot, he took the piece of sackcloth from beneath the pillow and then hurried back out, passing between the benches and entering the women's cabin, closing the door behind.

He went across to the far corner and laid the cloth on Oneesha's pillow. Reaching back, he withdrew the pair of stick figures and rested them beside, taking a moment to arrange them.

Satisfied no more was to be done, Isaac quickly made for the door. Stepping out, he turned to shut it after him.

'What you been doing in there, nigger?'

He jumped at the sound of Silas' voice and turned to face his approach.

The farmhand was holding the bowl of his pipe as he drew on the contents and regarded Isaac. 'I done asked you a question,' he stated.

'I be doing nothing, Boss.'

'You be doing nothing,' repeated Silas dubiously as he exhaled. 'It looks to me like you've gone and got yourself all in a muddle. That there is the cabin for the nigger tail. This here be the one for you,' he said, nodding sideways at the men's dormitory.

'Yessir.'

'So, I'll ask you again. What business do you have in there?' He held Isaac's gaze.

'None, Boss.'

'Now, that ain't quite what I'm getting at and you know it,' he stated, wagging the mouth of the pipe at him in reproach.

'Yessir. I just be looking for someone, is all.'

Silas' brows lifted and his lop-sided grin broadened, revealing his yellow teeth. 'Isaac, you ole devil you,' he said with a chuckle. 'I do believe you've got yourself some tail.'

He didn't respond.

'Tell me, does she call out your name when you take her to the gallop?'

Isaac bowed his head and stared at the ground.

'Looks like it's your turn,' stated Silas, lifting his left boot and tapping out the spent contents of the pipe on the heel.

Isaac looked over his shoulder to see Pete walking between the buildings with Oscar trailing behind. The look on the other slave's face was one of nauseated terror and he would not meet his gaze.

'Into the cabin,' instructed Pete before turning to him. 'Come with me.'

The farmhand turned and Isaac followed after watching Oscar enter the men's dormitory. His stomach began to churn with nervousness, the haunted look still held within his mind's eye.

As they rounded the corner he glanced back, his tension rising as he saw Silas open the door to the women's cabin, the scene then hidden from sight. He turned his gaze to Pete's back, his thoughts echoing the churning of his stomach as he wondered what lay ahead and whether Silas would spy what he'd left behind for Oneesha.

19

They approached the small shack at the rear of the cotton store that was usually used for tools and oddments. The door was wide open.

As Isaac drew closer he could see that a table had been placed inside with two chairs opposite each other. On the near chair sat a man with his back to the door. He wore a black suit despite the stifling heat, a pall of tobacco smoke rising about the rim of his dark Stetson.

Pete came to a halt beside the doorway and turned to him. Isaac hesitated, looking at the farmhand with uncertainty, unsure if he should wait to be asked in.

'Enter,' stated the man seated inside, his voice rough and deep.

He stepped up into the shack.

'Sit,' the man extended his hand to indicate the seat on the far side of the small table.

Isaac moved forward, seeing a sheet of paper and hammer lying on the table before the man. He seated himself, feeling a growing sense of apprehension.

'And your name is?' asked the man without looking up, taking up a pen laying beside the paper, the nib hovering in readiness as he took a drag on the hand-rolled cigarette hanging from his mouth.

'Isaac,' he replied, noting the metal collar tips on the man's white shirt that were decorated with the star of Texas, a narrow black tie hanging between.

He made a mark on the paper and slowly looked up as he exhaled, face obscured by smoke as he regarded Isaac with a steady gaze, narrow eyes filled with cold light. His square jaw was clean shaven, the sunlight slanting at his back casting pale shadows in his pock-marked and rugged skin.

Smoothing his chin, he made a soft clicking sound with his tongue as he pondered and continued to look across the tabletop. Isaac sat motionless, filled with tension as he was scrutinized in expectant silence.

'Where are my manners?' said the man with startling volume, slapping his leg and shaking his head in self-admonishment.

Isaac blanched in response, muscles taut with nervousness.

'Let me introduce myself. I'm Hale Owens. Your Master has instructed me to conduct an investigation into the murder of his daughter, who you knew as Miss Lilly. This here…,' he raised the sheet of paper, 'is a manifest of all the slaves working on the plantation.'

Owens rested the paper back on the tabletop and turned his attention to the hammer as the cigarette hanging from his lips smouldered. 'And this here is a hammer,' he said, taking it by the handle and lifting it. 'I wear it on one hip and my pistol on the other. I'm kinda famous for it.' He smiled to himself.

'Don't be fooled though. This ain't no ordinary hammer.'

Isaac looked at him questioningly.

'This here is a truth hammer. It helps me uncover the truth even when people ain't wishing to part with it.'

Owens laid the hammer down and leant back against the chair, which creaked slightly. Settling himself, he drew on the cigarette and crossed his legs casually, resting his hands on the upper knee.

'Now, I'm going to be asking you some questions and I want you to tell me the truth,' he said, smoke drifting from his mouth as he spoke.

'Yessir,' nodded Isaac.

'Before I begin, there's something you should know,' he stated. 'Folks who know me call me "Blood Hound"

Hale. You see, I have this…' He looked thoughtfully to the side as he took another drag. '…skill,' he finished with an exhale, turning his gaze back to Isaac. 'I suppose some might call it a talent, a real nose for the work. I can sniff out a lie like a hound sniffs out a runaway.'

Owens paused, leaning forward with slow deliberation, the chair creaking its accompaniment. He held Isaac's gaze as he rested his hand on the hammer.

'If I smell the slightest trace I'm going to set to work on you with this here hammer. First, I'll break your fingers one by one. Then, I'll shatter your ankles. By that point your tongue'll be looser than a Texas whore, but to be sure you ain't withholding, I'll mangle what you have between your legs. When you're done spilling everything there is to spill, I'll take the hammer to your skull because you won't be any damn use to anyone anymore.

'If I smell a lie, I smell blood.' He sat motionless for a few moments, hand remaining on the hammer, stare unwavering.

'I guess that's another reason why folks call me Blood Hound Hale,' he said, expression softening as he sat back once again. 'I like to get my hands dirty, so to speak.' He smiled across the table.

Isaac felt the hairs on the nape of his neck prickle. It was the coldest smile he'd ever set eyes on, filled with malice and a sense of coming satisfaction.

'Now, let's see what you know,' said Owens as he turned to the door over his right shoulder and flicked the cigarette butt out into the sunlight, a thin trail of smoke left in its wake.

'I be knowing nothing, Boss,' said Isaac, licking his lips, mouth dry.

'I'll be judge of that.' Owens smoothed his chin. 'Have you seen or heard anything relating to Miss Lilly's murder?'

'No, Sir,' he stated, shaking his head vigorously.

'Not a whisper?'

'No, Sir.'

'Has anyone been acting out of the ordinary.'

'Out of the ordinary? No, Sir.'

'You ain't seen or heard one little thing?'

'No, Sir.'

'Anyone gone a wandering when they shouldn't?'

'No, Sir,' he replied, turning his gaze downward.

Owens banged his palm on the table dramatically, causing Isaac to flinch in surprise. 'There it is!' he exclaimed with a laugh.

Isaac nervously raised his gaze. 'There be what, Boss?'

'The scent of a lie.' His eyes sparkled. 'Who's been a wandering, boy?'

'I done seen no one a wandering,' he replied truthfully, only having found Anthony vacant from his duties early in the week and not having seen where he'd gone.

'Then why avert your gaze when I asked?'

'Avert?'

'You turned your eyes to this here table,' he replied, patting the wood. 'You know what that means?'

'No, Sir.'

'You're trying to hide something from me, even after I warned you what would happen if I sniffed out a lie.' His hand moved to the hammer, fingers stroking the handle, which was darkened by the stains of use.

Isaac watched the caress, feeling a chill at the tenderness apparent in the soft touch. 'I not be lying, Boss,' he said, voice unsteady and heart pounding, the tight walls closing in.

A moment passed.

Owens stood sharply, grasping the hammer and thumping it down on the table as his chair banged against the wall of the shack. 'What did I say to you, nigger?' he roared. 'No lies. Didn't I say that, didn't I warn you I could sniff them out?'

Isaac cowered in the face of the violence of his words and actions. 'Yessir,' he nodded, staring up with wide eyes, arms raised in readiness to protect himself from the assault he feared was about to be unleashed upon him.

Owens took a breath, posture loosening slightly. 'Put your hands on the table,' he instructed, his voice now level and calm.

'I not be lying to you, Boss. There be nothing to tell 'cause I done seen nothing to tell of, and that's the God's honest truth,' he pleaded.

'Put your hands on the table,' repeated Owens, his tone deepening.

'I be looking at the table 'cause I be fearful, is all. You scare me with all the talk of what you be doing if I be lying.'

'I won't be telling you again.'

Isaac swallowed. There was no hint of concession in Owens' eyes and it was clear he wasn't going to be satisfied until his instruction had been fulfilled.

Hands trembling, Isaac laid them upon the wood, the feel of the grain beneath accentuated as they became the focus of his existence, fingers twitching in expectancy.

Owens stared down at him for a moment, gaze not leaving his.

The hammer was swiftly raised and brought back down, Isaac closing his eyes in anticipation as he fought the urge to withdraw his hands, knowing that such action would only worsen his punishment. The head thumped down, the table juddering in response to the strength of the blow.

Isaac raised his lids to find that Owens had struck the wood between his hands, an indention marking where the implement had fallen. He looked up, wincing and still fearful of being struck. He found Owens staring back at him, hammer raised in readiness.

'The next won't miss,' he said coldly. 'Now, be a good nigger and tell me what you know.'

'I be telling the truth,' replied Isaac. 'I done see no one a wandering.' He held the man's gaze, certain that if he now admitted finding Anthony absent from his work there would be punishment to follow.

'What about you?'

'Me, Sir?' Isaac was taken aback by the question and felt a flush rise upon his cheeks, resisting the urge to look down.

Owens nodded. 'Have you been a wandering when you shouldn't?'

Oscar's fearful expression came to mind and the pounding of his heart became desperate. Could he have seen him leave or return when meeting with Oneesha?

Hot silence pressed in as they held each other's gaze, a bead of sweat creeping down his temple. His hands continued to rest on the table, fingers trembling and palpitations making him feel sickly and faint.

'Either you're a foolish nigger or a brave one,' said Owens, lowering the hammer. 'Though some folks would say they're one and the same.'

He took his seat once again, setting the hammer down on the tabletop between them. Removing his hat briefly, he wiped his brow, the first sign that he felt the oppressive heat within the shack. Isaac waited, wondering what the investigator would do next, hands still upon the wood.

'You can go,' said Owens with a dismissive wave over his shoulder towards the doorway.

Isaac was taken aback, remaining in station for a moment as if unable to remove his hands from the tabletop. He lifted them, seeing the dark marks of sweat left on the surface. They continued to shake, his pulse still high, but in decline.

He stood, legs feeling weak. Taking care with each step, Isaac moved to the door, taking deep breaths to offset the nausea agitating his stomach.

'Some folks call me Hale "The Hammer" Owens,' stated the investigator without turning, 'or "Hammer-hand" Hale.'

Isaac hesitated in the doorway, glancing back over his shoulder as the investigator took a pouch of tobacco from the inside pocket of his dark jacket and began to roll a cigarette.

'I prefer Blood Hound Hale,' he added, 'because I can *always* sniff out a lie.' There was an ominous tone to his final words, Isaac feeling a chill as he began to walk away unsteadily, Pete straightening from where he leant against the wall and moving to lead the way back to the cabin.

20

Oneesha entered the kitchens from the passage, finding Seyeh and Casius engaged in a conversation of whispers by the doors at the far end. Moving to the left, she rinsed the knife she was carrying in the pail of water resting on the counter, giving it a drying wipe with the cloth beside.

Moving to the counter running the length of the room, she placed the knife into a draw and then turned to Seyeh, intending to make her exit. The older woman indicated for her to wait with a downward glance and a nod.

Oneesha moved to a stool by the central table and seated herself, unable to hear the words passing between the pair in conference. She stared idly at the grain of the tabletop, her duties for the day done and nothing pressing calling her away.

Casius vacated the kitchens and Seyeh paused, lifting the hem of her apron and thoughtfully wiping her hands on it more through habit than need. She turned and walked over, a serious expression upon her rounded face.

'Casius done leant his ear to the drawing room door this last evening, when Master Canyon was speaking with the investigator,' she said. 'Hale Owens be his name.'

Oneesha nodded as Seyeh continued to wipe her hands, the activity revealing her nervous tension.

'He wished he could speak with me earlier, but this be the first chance he had. We could have done warned the men if we had known.'

'Warned?' Oneesha stared up at Seyeh, her pulse rising.

'It be a warning and a reassurance of sorts.'

Oneesha's brow furrowed as she took a steadying breath and hoped that Isaac wasn't at risk of coming to harm. 'What be your meaning?'

'Owens were to interview the men today and will interview the women tomorrow. It be hoped he be finding clues as to the killing of Miss Lilly,' replied Seyeh. 'He were told not to damage the Master's property beyond use,' she added, looking at her meaningfully.

Oneesha cocked her head to the side, not comprehending what the older woman was trying to tell her.

'Slaves be the property he be speaking about.'

She nodded with eventual understanding.

Seyeh looked to the door through which Oneesha had entered, her hands still being wrung against the apron. 'Casius say Owens be a man from which nothing can be hid, that he be able to read thoughts just by looking into your eyes.'

Oneesha reached out and stilled the older woman's hands. 'Why you be worrying so? You got nothing to hide.'

Seyeh looked down, worry apparent in her tight expression. 'I done dropped three eggs on the floor just the other day and stole some of the persimmon brandy to help Rose sleep after what Silas did. Then there be the chicken and oat cakes...'

Her words trailed away as Oneesha shook her head, stifling a laugh.

'Why you be laughing at me?' she asked with confused surprise.

'Owens be here to investigate Miss Lilly's death, not to be finding out what you been doing in the kitchens.' She smiled warmly and squeezed Seyeh's hands. 'There be nothing for you to be worrying yourself about.'

Seyeh stood for a moment, the tension fading from her face. She nodded. 'You be right. I be fretting when I have no need.' She gave Oneesha's hands a squeeze in return.

'Will you walk with me back to the cabin?'

Seyeh shook her head. 'There still be things need doing here,' she replied with a glance about the kitchens.

Oneesha released the older woman's hands and stood. 'Then I be staying to help you.'

Seyeh lifted her hand to Oneesha's cheek. 'You be of help enough already. Go get some rest so you may be fresh come morning.'

'If you be sure.'

'Certain,' smiled Seyeh, lowering her hand.

Oneesha nodded, holding her gaze in fondness for a moment before turning and making her way over to the rear door.

'Will you be meeting with Isaac tonight?'

She looked over her shoulder and shrugged, unable to suppress the coy smile that arose. 'Mayhap I will, if fortune be in my favour.'

Seyeh chuckled. 'I hope it will bring its blessings,' she responded.

Oneesha opened the door and left the room, passing along the passage that was perpetually cool due to its location on the north side of the house. She stepped out and felt the temperature rise as she made her way to the cabin.

She entered to find a number of the other women already returned from their duties. Venus and Mitilde were stood by her cot and looked over with knowing grins as she walked over to join them.

They parted and Oneesha looked down at her pillow. Two figures made of twigs tied with grass lay side by side, their heads made of dirtied balls of cotton and their hands touching. Beside them was a piece of sackcloth bearing a depiction of the stick figures standing hand in hand beneath a large tree.

'It seems you done had a visitor,' commented Venus with a mischievous sparkle in her eyes.

Oneesha couldn't help but smile as she nodded.

'What do it mean?' asked Mitilde.

'He just saying he be thinking of me,' she replied, not willing to reveal the truth and feeling a little abashed in light of the other women's intrigued stares, cheeks flushed and gaze remaining on the items laying on the pillow.

Venus leant forward and looked at her face. 'I be thinking someone be in love,' she said with a chuckle.

'Be you in love?' asked Mitilde with excitement.

'Mayhap I am,' she conceded, the anticipation of the forthcoming meeting already building, the promise of seeing Isaac beneath the willow causing a lightness in her stomach which was filled with flutters of longing.

21

The stump tore loose, some of the surrounding earth crumbling and falling into the hole left in its wake. The workhorse dragged it a short distance before Pete brought it to a stop, his hand to the halter. Isaac and Oscar straightened, metal poles in their hands which had been used to lever the wood from its resting place.

Isaac wiped his brow with his forearm and glanced at the younger slave. They'd exchanged barely a word since arriving back at the west field, Pete always close at hand. He was clearly shaken and was unwilling to meet his gaze, head bowed and intent upon the work.

'That's it for the day, boys,' said Pete, glancing at the tree-line, the sun hidden beyond. 'Get this untied and we'll be on our way.'

Isaac moved around the shallow pit and went to the trunk, Oscar remaining a moment longer as her leant on his lever and recovered from the effort. He glanced along the track leading back to the plantation buildings as he bent to untie the rope. He'd been on edge ever since returning, expecting Silas to make an appearance and call him back for further questioning.

By the time Oscar drew up beside him, he'd undone the knots and the rope lay loose about the trunk, Pete untying the other end from the horse and letting the length fall to the dust. Isaac looked to Oscar's face, wanting to ask him about what may have been revealed to Hale Owens, but the farmhand remained close.

'Collect up the pail,' instructed Pete, nodding towards Isaac. 'Oscar, you lead Titan.'

Isaac walked over to the wall, picking up the pail and moving to the gateway as Pete went to his horse and mounted. The farmhand nudged his mount in the flanks and it set off at a sedate pace, moving past Isaac and onto the track. Oscar began to guide the workhorse, placing himself on the far side so the beast acted as a barrier.

Isaac waited until Titan had passed and then followed behind, strength sapped by the heat of the day and mentally weary due to the tense confrontation with Owens. His thoughts turned to Oneesha and he hoped she had found the items he'd left. He worried that Silas had discovered and disposed of them or that their presence had given him cause to approach her, providing him with the opportunity to make further advances.

The last thought caused the muscles of his jaw to stiffen and his pace to increase. He quickly drew alongside the workhorse and wished there were some way to encourage the farmhand to hurry, but knew any such suggestion would meet with a rebuke.

He pushed the aches of his body from his mind, a sense of dread growing with each passing moment. The journey drew out, time stretching and tortuous as he willed them to press on with greater haste.

The plantation buildings came into sight, the slave quarters obscured by the small copse of trees where Miss Lilly's swing hung empty and still. His gaze roamed the site, hoping for some sign that all was well. He noted a couple of farmhands languidly making their way northward along the track that ran alongside the men's dormitory and felt relief when he saw that one of them was Silas, able to discard his concern that Oneesha was in his unwanted company.

He heard the vague murmur of Silas' voice as he looked to their approach and then made comment to his companion.

'Perfect timing, Pete,' he called as he came to a stop at the fork where the west track met the north-south. 'Take these niggers over to the hole and haul the other one up out of there.'

'I ain't done had supper yet,' responded Pete unhappily.

'Well then, the quicker you be doing what I tell you, the quicker you'll be getting your fill.'

'Can't Jerry there take them on over?' he asked with a nod to the other man as the horse continued to draw steadily closer.

'It ain't be Jerry that I'm asking,' replied Silas pointedly. 'Now get your backside over to that hole and don't be filling my ears with no gripe.'

Pete frowned as he drew up before the other farmhands. 'Just be making sure ole White Cake don't eat all there is to be eaten. He's been worse then ever since he woke from the wilt.'

Silas walked over to Oscar and took hold of the workhorse's halter. 'I'll be taking that now, boy. You just a keep following Pete here.'

'Yessir.' He kept his head bowed.

Isaac and Oscar continued to follow behind the horse as they crossed straight over the junction and passed onto the patchy grass in the lea of the cotton store. It gave way to bare earth and the hole came into view, its narrow mouth unadorned and a length of rope lying coiled nearby.

Pete brought his horse to a stop. 'Get him up out of there,' he stated gruffly as he glanced round at them.

Isaac walked over with Oscar trailing. He picked up the length of rope and stepped up to the edge, looking down into the gathered gloom and spying Anthony's head and shoulders ten feet below, the hole barely a couple of feet across and allowing those assigned to its depths only enough room to stand.

'Anthony?' he called down, the volume of his voice stolen by the earth walls.

He looked up slowly, eyes reddened by lack of sleep.

'It be time for you to come up,' he stated, taking the hoop already tied at one end of the rope and lowering it down.

Anthony watched its steady progress and then took hold, passing it over his head and letting it sit under his arms. He looked back to Isaac and gave a nod.

'Oscar,' said Isaac with a nod to the tail end of the rope.

The young slave took it up and they began to heave. Their strength already much diminished by the labours of the day, they gritted their teeth with the effort, drawing Anthony up a hand's length at a time.

The top of his head appeared over the edge and he pulled himself out with a grunt of effort, collapsing onto the dirt and breathing deeply.

'On your feet, nigger. I ain't got all day to be waiting,' instructed Pete, wishing to get back to the bunkhouse and have his supper.

Anthony scowled at the farmhand as he lay in the dirt, his eyes filled with hatred.

'If you don't be getting up, there'll be another night in the hole for you,' stated Pete.

Anthony slowly got to his feet, letting the loop of rope fall down his body and come to rest about his feet.

'There's a good nigger,' said the farmhand condescendingly, giving the reins a gentle tug to the right and nudging the horse's flank with his heels.

Pete turned and began back along the side of the cotton store. Anthony took a step, stumbling and Isaac moving to his side to give his assistance.

He shrugged off the offered support with irritation. 'I don't need no help,' he hissed, glancing at Isaac coldly.

Silence lay between the three slaves as they followed behind the farmhand. Isaac could feel Anthony simmering

143

beside him and Oscar walked a couple of steps ahead with his head hanging low. There was nothing to be said, the dusk filled with the rub of crickets as night drew in.

22

The river was quickened and swollen by the rains that had passed north two nights previous, the bank broken in places and parts of the meadow's lower reaches flooded. The moon hung above the trees on the far side, a mere sliver of paleness affording little by way of illumination, its majority consumed by the darkness.

Oneesha waded through the grasses, a light mist beginning to rise. The willow loomed before her as a strange feeling arose within and she came to a halt. Her contemplative gaze turned inward as she sought out its source, an ominous chill causing her to tremble momentarily. It felt as though she were on the verge of some great event, that if she took one more step there could be no turning back from what lay waiting in the womb of the future, its birth in the present almost within reach.

Hesitating, she took a step forward, the sensation one of passing through an invisible barrier. The potential of the future had been born into the moment.

'Neesh.'

She blinked and looked to the willow, seeing Isaac step from its sheltered darkness, his features barely visible in the deep gloom. The feeling quickly fading into forgetfulness, she hid her right hand behind her back and began to make her way to him.

Isaac walked out to meet her and they stopped before each other. Oneesha smiled and took her hand from hiding, holding the posy out to him.

'The blossom of freedom,' she stated. 'They be the last of the persimmon blossoms.'

Isaac looked at the pale yellow flowers, each cupped in green leaves. He raised his gaze to hers once again in sudden realisation, recalling what he'd said to her on the night they'd last met. His eyes sparkled with tearful affection and he took the spray of twigs, a strip of blue cloth tied about their length. He was flooded with gratitude, her presence in his life a welcome counterpoint to the harshness of day to day existence and relieving the strain that still idled within after his confrontations with Silas and Owens.

'Seyeh tied the ribbon as I be all thumbs,' she stated, seeing the emotion in his eyes and taking hold of his free hand. 'Be you well?'

He nodded, choking back the tide. 'It be good to see you, is all.'

She looked at him with concern, seeking the truth in his shadowed gaze. 'You be sure?'

Isaac gave another nod of answer, remaining wordless as he continued to fight for composure, his weariness making him more susceptible to the whims of his feelings. He forced a smile and began to lead her to the willow, taking them into the deep darkness gathered about its trunk.

Bringing them to a halt, he turned to her and leant in, kissing her with heartfelt tenderness, arms passing around her and drawing her close as he retained his hold on the blossoms. They melted into each other in the darkness, two shadows becoming one beneath the still branches.

'I spoke with Cesar,' said Isaac softly when their lips parted and they stood in each other's arms. 'He say he be happy to wed us.'

'When?'

'On the morrow, if that be your wish.'

She glanced over his shoulder thoughtfully and then looked back to his eyes. 'It be my wish,' she said with a nod.

They kissed again and Isaac drew her down to the soil. Resting against the rough bark, she lay her head upon his shoulder and he leant his cheek against her hair after placing the posy on the ground beside him.

'Seyeh say the men be questioned by the investigator today.'

Isaac nodded and she felt the movement against the top of her head. 'He be a man I not wish to meet again.'

'He be questioning the women tomorrow,' she said, feeling him stiffen next to her in response to her words. 'There be no need to fret. Master Canyon has done told him to cause us no harm.'

'Truly?'

'Casius be a listening when he talk with the investigator and told Seyeh what he done heard.'

'Hale Owens be his name,' stated Isaac, 'though he like being called Blood Hound Hale.'

'"Blood Hound Hale"?' she repeated.

'He say he has a nose for lies and be able to sniff them out.'

She turned to look up at him. 'Seyeh say similar. She speak of him being able to read minds.'

'He be no mind reader, but a face reader,' he said. 'Be sure not to look down at the table after he ask a question. It be a sign of a lie, or so he say.'

She studied his deeply shadowed expression a moment. 'Did you look down?'

Isaac nodded again and looked out to the meadow.

'Was you lying?' she asked softly.

The rasping cries of crows suddenly arose in the night.

Isaac and Oneesha sat up quickly, looking to the trees rising from the strip of wilderness that followed the river south beyond the border of the meadow. Their eyes were wide with concern as they sought out the reason for the birds' alarm, the fluttering of wings in the branches adding to the disturbance.

'There!' exclaimed Oneesha in a whisper, pointing towards the field's entrance two hundred yards away.

Isaac followed her gaze and the hairs on the back of his neck prickled.

A dark figure was drifting down the rise, following the vague path that led to the river. The lower portion of its spectral form was obscured by the grasses as it moved in steady silence, the crows once more settling in the trees beyond.

'It be Mistress Canyon,' stated Oneesha in hushed surprise as the figure drew closer, veering towards the waters lying to the left and the thin mist gently stirring in its wake.

They watched as she moved to the bank with contemplative slowness. She came to a halt amidst the bull rushes, standing motionless and looking out over the swollen depths.

Not a breath of wind stirred. The hush pressed close as her dark presence muted all sound and drew in all light. She stood eerily still beside the waters, a spectre filled with brooding potency.

Isaac and Oneesha were held transfixed. They echoed her stillness, staring fearfully from beneath the tree, pulses racing and bodies tingling with unnerving chills.

They flinched as the screech of an owl sounded above the meadow, its flight hidden in the gloom.

The black figure of Mistress Canyon toppled forward, arms at her sides.

Oneesha gasped, Isaac jumping at the sound as the splash of her entry into the swift waters lifted into the night and they looked across the meadow in horror, temporarily held in place by the shock of what they'd witnessed.

Isaac leapt up and ran from the cover beneath the willow branches. The grasses sighed against his leggings as he rushed to where Mistress Canyon had been standing.

Oneesha rose to her feet and followed after him, lifting the hem of her nightshirt to allow greater haste. She reached his side and they looked to the river for any sign of their Mistress, the high waters lapping at the grass edging the bank.

'The current be strong,' commented Isaac as he peered downstream, the meagre light afforded by the moon hindering any hope of spying the woman amidst the flow.

Oneesha looked over her shoulder in alarm, staring towards the gateway. 'I think I be hearing the dogs,' she said in breathless fear.

Isaac turned and listened. Hounds bayed in the distance, their eager cries arising from the direction of the plantation buildings.

'They think we be runaways if they catch us.' Her eyes were wide with growing panic.

Isaac glanced at the river and a chilling realisation dawned. 'No, they think we be murderers.'

She looked at him, her gaze pleading for him to offer a solution to their terrifying predicament as the cries of the hounds grew louder.

'You must run,' he stated. 'Go to yonder trees and be making your way to the north field. From there you be able to get back to the cabin,' he said, nodding to the woods one hundred yards beyond the willow.

'Be you not coming with me?' she asked, despairing of being separated.

'I be drawing them off,' he replied as the baying drew ever closer.

She was aghast at his words. 'But…'

'This be no time for arguing, Neesh,' he said as he stepped over to her and gave her a kiss in an attempt at reassurance. 'I be seeing you soon. Now go!'

She held his gaze a moment longer, wishing to hold out her hand and draw him safely into the darkness.

'Go!' he insisted with pleading urgency, waving her away.

Oneesha turned and ran, her heart aching as she left her love standing on the riverbank and made for the darkened woods.

23

Isaac ran along the vague path, which was no more than a shadow curving through the grasses. Reaching its turn to the south, he spied the flames of torches and lanterns in the cotton field beyond. Hoping his scent would take the attention of the hounds, he turned back to the river, making for the wilderness at the meadow's southern end.

He passed into the scrub of trees and bushes. His heart pounding, he kept sight of the river to his left, the sound of branches rustling with his passage increasing his tension.

The baying of the hounds arose with renewed intensity and Isaac guessed that his scent had been discovered. He heard the call of men in the meadow at his back, their words indistinct but voices carrying in the stillness.

His teeth gritted, he put every effort into his flight. His legs ached as he drew on his reserves of strength, the work in the west field having left him with little to spur his steps over the uneven ground.

He leapt over a fallen free. A branch snapped beneath his feet as he landed on the far side. His shoulders tightened, sweat crawling down his temples as he ran on.

Isaac raised his arm as he pushed through a thicket blocking his way, his progress painfully slow as thorns drew bloody lines across his skin.

He glanced back as the crows took fright once again, rising from a copse to his right and signalling his whereabouts to those in pursuit. He saw flames through the darkness, the hounds crying out for his capture, but still on the leash.

Breaking from the clawing branches, he passed over a small stream, its mouth bloated by the flood waters. His feet sank into boggy ground, slipping on the slick grass as the dogs whined for release and their chance to give chase.

Throat burning, he skirted more bushes that appeared as thick shadows before him. He moved to the river bank, the sodden earth threatening to collapse beneath his weight. A clod was loosed by his passing and splashed into the waters, Isaac wincing in response to the sound.

He passed into a strand of trees. His left foot caught a root rising from the ground. He stumbled, losing the battle to retain his balance and falling with his hands outstretched before him.

Struggling to his feet in weary desperation, he continued on, his steps laboured and becoming increasingly heavy with effort.

'Well, look who we have here.' Hale Owens stepped from behind a tree ten yards ahead.

Isaac's heart leapt and he came to a halt. His mouth was thick with phlegm and his chest heaved with the strain of exertion.

'I'll be darned if it ain't Isaac the liar,' said Owens with amusement, drawing on his cigarette, the tip glowing and its light catching the malicious glint in his eyes.

Isaac's gaze settled on the pistol aimed at his chest. He glanced over his shoulder as the whining of the dogs ceased and their howls rose with chilling desire, signalling their release from restraint.

'It seems you're a fool after all.' Owens exhaled, the cloud of smoke lingering. 'It also seems I done caught me a murderer.'

Isaac heard the rapid sound of the hounds' approach through the undergrowth. His muscles taut and quivering, he stared at the man before him and gauged whether to make a lunge for the gun.

24

Oneesha scrambled from the wood by the rough fence that surrounded the slave burial ground in the top corner of the north field. Breathing heavily, she moved away from the gathering of wooden crosses that whispered of those that had gone before.

She began to pass the rows of cotton plants, heading south towards the plantation buildings that were still hidden by the lay of the land.

A gunshot rang out in the night.

She froze and stared south-east with wide eyes. The cries of the hounds fell away in the darkness, the furious thunder of her heart filling her chest as she trembled.

Listening intently, Oneesha's ears were filled with the rush of blood as she considered going back to the meadow. She heard the distant sound of men's calls drawing up from the riverside and decided to make good her journey to the slave quarters in the hope of finding Isaac waiting there.

She hurried up the rise before her, passing between the fence and cotton plants. The buildings came into sight as she began down the gentle slope beyond, looking to the lights that shone from the lower floor of the Big House. The cabins and sheds nestled to the right were deep in shadow and there was no sign of activity.

Her pace slowed and she stayed low, moving tighter to the fence in the hope it would help conceal her. The noise of her feet upon the soil caused her to wince with its apparent volume and she tried to lighten her steps.

Oneesha neared the end of the field and moved to one of the last avenues between the cotton plants, passing along its cool length, the thin mist that was gathering disturbed by her tentative movements. Reaching the end, she made for the nearby gateway.

She crouched by the post, looking east along the track beyond. Seeing no sign of torches or lanterns, she moved from the limited concealment and made her way to the right.

Passing onto the north-south track, Oneesha kept to its edge. She made for the cluster of sheds and barns, reaching the front of the cotton store and creeping alongside the wooden slats.

She saw movement and became still. Her pulse quickened as she stared along the track. Dark figures were loitering near the far end of the men's cabin, the Spanish moss in the copse of trees on the other side of the track swaying slightly.

One of the figures began to move forward and she recognised the waddling gait immediately.

'Neesh?'

'It be me,' she said, straightening and slowly walking towards the older woman.

'What you be doing here?' asked Seyeh as they halted before each other.

'I were meeting with Isaac. Be he back?'

Seyeh's expression fell and she shook her head. 'They took the dogs out and we be hearing their cries,' she said, glancing over her shoulder at the other slaves who had been roused from their beds by the commotion. 'There were a gunshot.'

Oneesha nodded, turning back to stare at the fork in the track that led east, her stomach churning. She feared the worst and considered returning to the meadow once again, an image of Isaac fending off the hounds stirring in her mind's eye and giving her a chill, the hairs on her arms rising.

'They say Mistress Canyon could not be found and Master Canyon called for Silas to go a searching.'

'We saw her,' responded Oneesha distractedly, willing Isaac to come into view.

'Saw her, where?'

'Down by the river. She done fall into the waters.' She took a wavering breath, nausea rising.

'She fall?'

Oneesha turned her attention back to the older woman and nodded again. 'She stood awhile as we be watching from under the willow.'

'Be she dead?'

'We not be seeing her when we looked from the bank. Then we hear the dogs and...' She shook her head, tears gathering in her eyes as she swallowed back. 'We be separated,' she stated with a despairing tone.

The whine of a hound arose in the stillness and they looked to the east track.

'They be coming back,' stated Seyeh, taking hold of her hand and dragging her to where the small gathering of slaves restlessly waited.

The sound of men's voices followed behind and when they reached the others they turned to see Silas leading a knot of farmhands onto the north-south track, the hounds on their leashes, held in pairs by two of the men. Their torches flickered, lanterns hung on the end of rifles and shotguns.

Oneesha spied a body being carried between two of the men to the rear of the group, but was unable to identify who it was. She took a step forward in order to gain a better view, but Seyeh retained her grip on her hand.

Silas saw the slaves on the track, one of the dogs barking and growling threateningly. 'Marsha,' he snapped, turning to the hound.

The man holding her leash gave it a sharp tug and she whined in pained response before falling silent.

'What in the Lord's name are you niggers doing out here?' called Silas as the farmhands drew close, raising the lantern he was carrying into the air and scanning their faces.

'Get back into them there cabins. There ain't nothing for you to be seeing here and I won't be hearing any griping about not getting rest when the day comes, unless you be fixin' for time in the hole.'

The slaves began to drift back to the dormitories. Seyeh gave Oneesha's hand a gentle tug, but she planted her feet and would not move until she'd seen whose body was being carried amidst the farmhands.

She moved to the side of the track as they neared, staring through them, breathless and taut with fearful expectation. Seyeh moved with her, faithfully remaining by her side, her grip on Oneesha's hand tightening in betrayal of her own tension.

Oneesha's expression became one of horror as her gaze settled on the face of the figure sagging between the two farmhands. It was a pool of gory darkness, the nose and skull caved in.

She looked to the body, narrowing her eyes as she sought out its identity. A flood of relief rushed through her when she noted metal collar tips glinting in the torchlight, the shirt to which they were attached darkened by blood.

Silas looked at the two women as he drew alongside. 'You best be getting back inside if you know what's good for you,' he snarled.

He came to a halt a couple of steps further down the track and turned back to them, raising the lantern to Oneesha's face. 'Well, ain't this a happy coincidence?' he said, grin curling his lips.

She looked at him in puzzlement.

'I have news about your man,' he stated with vindictive satisfaction as the other farmhands continued past.

Her eyes widened as she stared at him, her nausea renewed.

'What be your news?' enquired Seyeh nervously, Oneesha unable to find voice.

Silas glanced at the older woman and then turned back to Oneesha. 'He's dangling from a rope down by the river.'

She fought for air, drawing it in through flaring nostrils. The tightness of her chest was crushing, her heart desperate against her ribcage. Her legs became weak as Silas held her gaze, his grin broadening.

He leant towards her, bringing his face close enough that his smoky breath brushed against her face. 'And ain't nobody going to be taking him down,' he said, voice low and threatening. 'He's going to stay up in that there willow for the crows to feast on.'

Her expression became desolate, mouth falling open.

'A murderer don't deserve any better,' stated Silas, taking a step back.

Holding her gaze a moment longer, he then set off after the other men, who had vanished from sight around the end of the cabin. Oneesha continued to stare straight ahead, body trembling.

Her legs gave way and she began to fall, Seyeh quickly gathering her into her arms.

'Pete,' called Silas as he reached the far end, 'make sure these two niggers here get back to their cabin.' He glanced back with a sneer and then stepped from sight.

'Isaac,' whispered Oneesha as Pete walked around the corner of the building, a torch in one hand and rifle in the other.

'You two! Get back to your cabin or you'll be spending time in the hole,' he barked.

'Come,' said Seyeh softly, having to bear Oneesha's stricken form towards the waiting farmhand.

They passed him and he followed a few yards behind as they made their way over to the women's dormitory. Gratefully entering the darkness, Seyeh shut the door with one arm about Oneesha, who leant against her as if without a will of her own.

Moving over to Oneesha's cot, Seyeh seated her on the edge, keeping a hand to her shoulder for fear she would topple without support.

'Should I be staying with you?' she whispered.

Oneesha nodded vaguely, the gesture almost lost in the deep gloom.

She tentatively released her shoulder, Oneesha remaining seated as the older woman pulled back the cover. Seyeh lifted her legs into the bed, her body turned by the motion and falling slowly until her head rested on the pillow.

Oneesha turned to face the wall and shifted to the far side.

Seyeh looked down at her momentarily and then climbed in beside, drawing the cover over them and placing her arm about the young slave. She thought to offer words of consolation, but found none forthcoming.

She held her close and felt the tremors that hinted at the tears that were being shed in the darkness as Oneesha began to cry. She began to stroke her hair as they lay together on the cot, the dark silence heavy with grief.

25

The faintest touch of grey light was visible through the cracks of a dried knot in the wood before her face. Oneesha felt Seyeh's soft breathing against her back, the older woman's arm draped over her as she slept.

She lifted it from her midriff and turned carefully, setting it down on Seyeh's wide hips. Grasping the bed cover along its length, she pulled it back and sat up. The cot creaked and she stiffened, glancing down to check the minor disturbance hadn't caused wakefulness.

Satisfied that Seyeh still slept, she manoeuvred herself to the foot of the cot and then climbed over the older woman's legs, holding her nightshirt up and taking every care not to brush against her skin. Her bare feet came to rest on the floorboards and she stood, looking down upon the kindly woman, who groaned in her sleep, smacking her lips together momentarily.

She made her way to the door, passing Seyeh's empty cot and stepping out into dawn's first light. Moving by the men's cabin, she heard snoring within as she turned to the right and made for the track that would take her east.

Oneesha reached the fork and took the turn with growing trepidation, dampened dust clinging to her soles as if attempting to discourage her from making the journey. She tried to bolster herself for what was to come, to prepare for the sight that awaited in the hush, knowing in truth that no amount of forethought could lessen the impact of its reality.

She passed into the meadow. The cold light of dawn was diffused by a blanket of mist shrouding the wide river, bull rushes ghostly and still upon its near bank. Amidst the rough grasses stood the solitary willow, faint creaking issuing from its secretive shadows and creeping into the gathered hush. Tendrils of mist drifted above the bare earth at the foot of its wide trunk and a figure hung from one of the boughs above, gently swaying to and fro.

She approached through the paleness, a shadow in a dream. Her cheeks glistened, eyes filled with loss and speaking of a heart wrung tight by the sight revealed beneath the looming tree.

She fell to her knees, the grasses caressing her skin with the moisture of fading night. Her weeping was woven into the mist as she covered her face, bent and bowed by the weight of her grief.

'Oneesha.' The word sighed through the meadow.

She lifted her head and turned to the river, inhaling deeply, the breath staggered by her weeping. 'The river calls me.'

Her gaze was attracted by movement and she saw a dark silhouette rising amidst the rushes, for a moment fearful that it was Mistress Canyon returned to claim her for the waters.

'Neesh.'

The whisper contained a tone she recognised, but dare not believe was real.

'It be Isaac.' He stepped from the partial concealment, glancing at the entrance to the field before making his way over to her.

'Isaac,' she said breathlessly, getting to her feet and watching his approach, her astonishment keeping her steadfast.

He came to a halt a few yards from her as crows began to caw in the waking stillness.

'I thought it be you hanging in the tree,' she said softly, lacking the courage to reach out and touch his cheek for fear he would vanish into the mist, merely a figment of her imagination.

Isaac shook his head, briefly looking to the willow before stepping forward and embracing her. Oneesha wilted into him, head upon his shoulder and lifting her arms to hold him with needy tightness.

'I thought you be dead,' she sobbed, relief overpowering her.

They stood entwined for long moments. A toad's deep call arose from the grasses nearby, receiving a response from nearer the river as the day slowly brightened.

Her tears abating, a realisation came upon Oneesha and she lifted her head to stare into his eyes. 'Who be hanging in the tree?'

'Anthony.'

'Anthony!' She looked at him in surprised bewilderment.

He looked out across the meadow thoughtfully. 'Owens done confront me as I ran,' he began. 'The dogs was off the leash and I thought it be my time for the grave.

'Anthony charged from the brush and leapt upon him. He done pulled the hammer from Owens' belt and stove his head in.'

'Hammer?' Oneesha's brow furrowed. 'I be hearing a gunshot.'

He turned his gaze to her. 'He be carrying a hammer on one hip and pistol on the other. He let off a shot and winged Anthony as he be bearing down on him.

'The dogs was close and I climbed a tree as Anthony beat down again and again. There I sat as the dogs came leaping and biting below. The men came and he be beaten and dragged away.

'He done saved my life and be giving up his own to do it.'

She raised a hand to his cheek and cupped it gently. 'I be glad of it,' she whispered, looking at him with deep affection as she stroked his skin with her thumb.

'We should back to the cabins before the farmhands find you gone,' she said after a few moments had passed, her hand falling away from his face as she stepped from his arms.

'They be not knowing?'

Oneesha shook her head. 'They do no count. Mayhap they think they done caught the killer and there be no need, but if we not hurrying then they be waking the men and soon discover you be gone.'

He took hold of her hand. 'We best wait to be wed,' he said regretfully as they began to make their way back to the plantation buildings.

She nodded, wishing that it wasn't so, but knowing that the events of the night would cast a shadow over their union should they be joined by Cesar that day. They would wait until life had settled back into its routine, until the violent and vivid memories had been subdued by the languid heat of the days to come.

26

She sat before the wash tub rubbing a pair of britches on the scrubbing board leant against the near rim. The sun's warmth lay upon Oneesha as she worked, rocking back and forth and expression tight as she tried to remove the grime caked into the brown corduroy. There was no scent to the water, which was frothed with a plain soap used when washing the farmhands' clothing.

Oneesha made every effort to concentrate on the task, trying not to dwell on what had occurred during the night and the sight which had stricken her before Isaac had revealed his presence by the river. The shadow of Anthony's body hung in the back of her mind, its gentle swinging calling her thoughts back to the disturbing image.

'Seyeh be taking her time,' commented Mitilde.

Oneesha was given a start by the young slave's voice. She turned to the girl kneeling to her right, another tub resting between them where Seyeh would take up station. The older woman had gone to collect up the last of the dirty washing from the bunkhouse and had yet to return, the sun having risen over the Big House in the time she had been gone.

'Mayhap she were called away to some other duty,' she responded, yawning and blinking away the tears that gathered in her shadowed eyes.

They worked in silence for a time, Oneesha finishing with the britches and taking a shirt from the basket beside her, the smell of body odour wafting to her as she took it beneath the water and kneaded it against the bottom of the tub.

'Do you think he kill them?' asked Mitilde, glancing over and voice soft as she scrubbed a shirt on her wash board.

The darkened figure swung, its metronomic movement calling her inner gaze back to its ghoulish presence. 'Mayhap he did, mayhap he didn't. It make no difference now,' she replied, frown deepening.

'I think he be heading off to the Union,' said the young slave with a nod to herself. 'The investigator just happened upon him by the river, is all.'

'I be hearing no more talk of this now, Mitty,' she responded snappily. 'Set your mind to the work and leave such things for cabin talk.'

172

Mitilde glanced over again, surprised by the manner of Oneesha's response. She usually welcomed talk at the tubs and the unusual reaction piqued the young slave's curiosity, one she hoped to satiate with further enquiries at a later time.

They continued to work, the sun beating down on them and the cool water within the tubs bringing a little relief. Oneesha felt weary, the sleepless night staining her eyes and tainting her mood with melancholy.

Seeing movement in the periphery of her vision, she looked up, her expression registering surprise. Walking around the side of the Big House was Silas with Master Canyon to the left dressed in his suit of mourning, two farmhands flanking to the rear. Their strides were filled with purpose as they crossed the lawn towards the tubs and she lowered the shirt into the water.

'Mitilde,' she said, alerting the younger woman to the small company drawing close as she got to her feet and smoothed the apron hanging over her pale blue dress.

Straightening and turning her full attention to their approach, she inwardly recoiled when she saw their bitter expressions. Their jaws were set and there was a distinct sense of hostility as they came to a halt a few yards away.

'Pete,' said Silas over his left shoulder, 'bind her hands.'

The farmhand stepped over towards Mitilde. Oneesha looked to the young slave, wondering what she could have done to warrant such treatment.

Mitilde cowered, taking an involuntary step back.

Pete walked around her, a length of rope in his hands. Surprise registered on her face as he continued along the short line of tubs towards Oneesha, who blanched at his unexpected approach.

'Hold out your hands,' he stated as he stopped before her.

'What have I done?'

'I ain't gonna be asking you again,' he growled.

Oneesha did as instructed and Pete bound her wrists, making sure the bond was secure with a rough tug.

Grasping the top of her arm with painful tightness, he led her back the way he'd come, passing behind Mitilde, who stood as if in a daze. The farmhand drew her to a stop before the other men and Master Canyon regarded her with a look of burning hatred. She winced beneath its heat, filled with confusion.

'To the bunkhouse,' said Silas, turning and leading the group back across the lawn.

Oneesha was propelled forward with a shove. She glanced back at Mitilde questioningly, but the young slave simply looked on in amazement as she stood behind her wash tub.

They walked around the corner of the Big House and went to the front of the bunkhouse resting to the right. Four horses were tied to the wooden railing that fronted the simple porch, another farmhand standing in the doorway with a rifle in the crook of his arm.

Silas walked to the nearest mount, taking a coil of rope that hung from the pommel of the saddle in readiness. Tying it to the horse, he walked to her with its slack trailing in the dirt.

Pete continued to hold onto her as Silas tied it about her forearms above the bonds which already restrained her. She looked to his face, seeking clues as to why she was being treated in such a way and seeing only determination.

'Why you be doing this?' she asked as he straightened.

Master Canyon stepped up and Silas moved aside. He looked upon her in disgust, his body trembling slightly and the threat of his presence causing her to wilt as his eyes continued to blaze.

With shocking suddenness, he struck her across the cheek with the back of his hand. Her head was whipped to the side, eyes watering and jaw aching with the force of the blow.

'Take her to the willow,' he barked, turning and walking to the horses.

He four men mounted, Oneesha finding it hard to breathe as Silas led her past the slave quarters and onto the track beyond.

Silas brought them to a stop, turning to Master Canyon, who nodded in answer to the silent question that passed between them. He whipped the reins and kicked his heels into the horse's flanks. It whinnied and set off at a gallop.

Oneesha was yanked from her feet and dragged behind, her screams rising with the dust. Master Canyon and the two farmhands set off after them, the sounds of hoofs pounding the ground mingling with her cries of suffering.

Seyeh wrung her hands upon her apron as she sat in the women's dormitory and heard the terrible sounds, face pinched with her own mental anguish. 'Can I be leaving now?' she asked.

The farmhand standing by the door looked at her and shook his head. 'I was told to keep you here and here's where I'll be keeping you until told otherwise.'

'But there be duties I must attend to.'

He ignored her protest, turning his attention to rolling a cigarette, taking a pouch of tobacco and some papers from his britches as he leant against the door.

Seyeh stared at him and then looked to the shuttered window before her as she remained seated on one of the cots in the middle of the cabin. Her hands continued to wring out her distress as the sounds of Oneesha's departure echoed within her mind and she bowed her head, offering up a prayer for mercy.

27

Isaac turned the spade, letting the soil upon its head spill onto the pile beside him. He paused and wiped perspiration from his brow before continuing, he and Oscar having to spend additional time digging deeper about a tree stump that was stubbornly retaining its hold on the ground.

The blade sliced down and he pressed his hardened sole to it before bending with the motion of taking up another heap of earth. He glanced at Wilson as he tipped the load to the side, the farmhand returned to his duties and watching with disinterest as he leant against Titan twenty yards away.

The blade sliced down again, the jarring of its rest loosing a bead of sweat from his nose. He looked up and turned to Oscar with a curious expression, the young slave to his left working relentlessly.

'Did you be hearing that?' he asked.

'What?' replied Oscar without turning, shovelling up the dirt and flinging it to the side as he uncovered a large root.

'I thought I done hear screaming.' Isaac looked to the entrance, his gaze following the track beyond.

'I be hearing no such thing. Your mind be playing tricks,' stated the young slave, putting down his spade and taking up the felling axe that had been lying in the dust.

Isaac felt the urge to return to the plantation buildings arise within him as he continued to stare down the track with a look of puzzlement. 'I be sure it were screaming.'

'It be but a bird and you hear it with a tired mind, is all,' said Oscar dismissively as he swung the axe.

'Get back to work, Isaac,' called Wilson, Titan shifting beside him and whipping his tail to usher away the flies settling on his rump.

He sliced the spade down into the earth distractedly. The feeling to return could not be shaken and he wondered at its origin as he took up the broken soil and tipped it beside him, a few stray clods falling back into the hole.

'Watch your work,' said Oscar under his breath as he hacked at the root, skin glistening in the sunlight.

Shaking his head, Isaac pushed the sensation aside and dug deep, stamina sapped by tiredness and the heat of the day. He thought about Oneesha and made note to talk with Cesar about being wed the following week, smiling thinly to himself as he laboured in the rippling haze.

28

Oneesha was raised to her feet with rough impatience, her head bowed and trails of tears darkening the dust upon her face. The skin of her underarms and shins was tatty and bloodied, the wounds thick with grime. Her apron had been torn away during the journey to the meadow, the dress beneath now ragged and filthy.

Silas undid the bond that had been used to drag her to the meadow and held her upper arm, keeping on her feet. She quaked with fear as they stood before the willow, the creaks of Anthony's swinging corpse cutting into her like sharpened blades.

'Pete, you climb on up there and tie the rope,' he instructed with a nod towards the tree. 'Jerry, get her up on Patty.'

'I ain't gonna have no dirty nigger sitting on my saddle,' complained the farmhand in response.

'It ain't as if she's going to be sitting on it long,' responded Silas as Pete took up the length of rope and coiled it before walking over to the trunk.

'Long or short ain't the point,' said Jerry.

'Then take the saddle off,' said Master Canyon with irritation as he stood to the left, his horse grazing on the long grasses at his back.

'She ain't going to be worrying about comfort,' commented Silas. 'At least, not for long,' he added, turning and sneering at her.

The gesture was lost on Oneesha as she stared at the ground. She was filled with confusion and fear, her mind in turmoil as she tried to fathom what was happening to her.

Jerry unfastened the saddle as Pete climbed along the limb from which Anthony hung, passing over the swaying body and then sitting astride the bough in the dappled shadows. He tied a noose in one end of the rope and secured the other about the branch before letting it drop, jumping down after it.

The thud of his landing made Oneesha flinch and look up. Her gaze settled on the rope, eyes widening and legs buckling as she swooned, Silas retaining his grip and keeping her standing.

Pete bent by the trunk, picking up the posy of blossoms lying upon the ground.

'What you got there, Pete?' asked Silas.

'Looks like she brung him some flowers,' replied the farmhand, dropping them before him and crushing them under boot.

'More proof,' said Silas, turning to Master Canyon. 'Not that we be needing any.'

The plantation owner nodded, wiping his face with a handkerchief as he waited for his vengeance to be satisfied.

'Get her up on the horse,' stated Silas propelling her towards Jerry as he stood beside his mount.

Oneesha collapsed against the farmhand, who pushed her away violently, sending her tumbling to the ground. Pete strode over and the two of them lifted her up, taking her to the horse.

'You be a good little nigger and climb on up there,' said Jerry with a snarl.

She stood dumb, an emptiness howling within her, thoughts spinning around its dark vacancy.

The pair of farmhands looked at each other in annoyance as she remained unmoving before them, her body trembling. They took hold of her and hefted her onto the horse's back, sitting her up before Jerry led the creature beneath the still boughs.

He moved past the noose and turned the horse around, bringing it to a halt with the rope hanging before Oneesha's face. Climbing up behind her, he passed it over her head, tightening it and giving it a pull to make sure it was secure.

'I tied it good and tight,' stated Pete as he watched.

Oneesha's gaze fell on the entrance to the meadow at the top of the rise. She longed for Isaac to come into view, to see him one last time within the long grasses of the meadow where they'd danced and their hearts had been free.

Silas turned to Master Canyon, who simply nodded in response to the silent question being asked. The head farmhand moved beneath the branches as Jerry jumped off his horse, making his way from beneath the willow with Pete beside him.

Moving to the rear of the beast, Silas raised his right hand as a single tear rolled down Oneesha's cheek and she continued to look for her love.

A moment passed.

He gave the horse's rear and stinging slap and it trotted forward. Oneesha was briefly drawn along it back and then dropped with a gasp.

The rope pressed against her windpipe with sudden violence, crushing it with her own weight. She choked for breath, legs kicking and bound hands curled into fists. Her eyes bulged as she looked to the emptiness of the entrance, heart aching and lungs filled with bursting pain.

Oneesha's tongue lolled from her mouth as she coughed and spluttered, the rope slowly turning with the movements of her legs. Her sight was taken to the river, the sunlight upon its surface glittering faintly in her watery eyes.

Silas walked away without a backward glance, Jerry already leading his horse towards the river in order to wash down its back before replacing the saddle. Master Canyon stood and watched as Silas and Pete mounted, both looking to him as they waited to return to the plantation buildings.

Oneesha stopped struggling as she stared at the ribbons of shimmering light, a strange sense of calm pervading her. The river called her onward, promising to take her to the ocean, to carry her safely across the threshold in its arms.

She closed her eyes in acceptance of its invitation. The sound of horses moving away was heard at the edge of her hearing as all faded to darkness and Oneesha slipped from consciousness.

29

Isaac rounded the end of the men's cabin with Oscar beside him, Wilson already striding towards the bunkhouse after griping about his hunger during the journey back from the west field. Seyeh was seated on the nearest of the benches and burst into tears as soon as she set eyes on him, rising and hurrying over.

She fell upon her knees before him and gathered his hands into hers. 'Forgive me,' she begged, words thick with emotion and cheeks awash with tears. 'Please forgive me.'

He looked to Oscar questioningly, the young slave shrugging.

Turning back to Seyeh, he was unsure how to respond as she wept and wailed at his feet, holding his hands to her forehead. 'What be there to forgive?' he asked, disquieted by her attentions.

She looked up at him, top lip glistening with mucus that streamed from her nose, eyes raw and pleading. 'I not be meaning for any harm to come to her,' she said, sniffing and wiping her face with a forearm.

Nausea immediately came upon him. 'Where's Oneesha?' he asked, breaking into a cold sweat and chest tight.

Seyeh bowed her head, her soulful weeping renewed as Oscar remained watchful nearby.

Isaac glanced to the women's cabin as his pulse raced and then turned back to her. He crouched, withdrawing his hands from hers and taking hold of her shoulders. 'Where be Neesh?' he asked, panic beginning to rise.

She lifted her gaze, expression filled with anguish. She shook her head, trying to speak but finding herself unable, letting out a cry from her depths and face contorting.

'Seyeh,' he said firmly, gripping her shoulders tightly. 'You must tell me where she be?'

She fought for breath and control, struggling to contain the swell of emotion. 'In the hanging tree,' she managed between gasps.

Isaac looked at her in horror. 'The willow?' he asked, swallowing against the rising sickness. 'When?'

She nodded. 'They think she in league with Anthony,' she sniffed, looking into his eyes. 'I never meant her no harm. She be like a daughter to me.'

'When she be taken, Seyeh?' he reiterated with urgency.

'I done found it in the washing basket,' she said, tears spilling down her cheeks, the urge to plead her innocence holding back her sobs. 'It were tucked into Silas' britches and so I ask him where he get Miss Lilly's handkerchief.'

Isaac's grip on her shoulders weakened as he recalled the screams he'd heard while in the west field, knowing with chill certainty that they'd been those of his love. 'It be too late,' he stated, heart rent apart by the thought that he did not go to Oneesha's aid, that his moment had passed.

'He take me to Master Canyon and done tell him he see Oneesha returning to the cabins with a man late one night, but he not see who.' She sniffed and wiped her nose again, regaining a degree of self-control.

Isaac looked to her, eyes despairing as he remained silent and struggled to come to terms with his sense of guilt.

'When Anthony done went for Silas at the well, he come to thinking he be the man returning with Oneesha. They think he be a waiting for her when they find him down by the river last night,' she stated, taking a steadying breath.

'The handkerchief?' he asked in a whisper.

'It be proof she done knew he killed Miss Lilly,' she replied, 'along with Mr Owens, Mistress Canyon and that woman found in the woods too.'

'Mistress Canyon,' he echoed, shaking his head, but unable to find the will to explain the truth of the woman's demise.

Isaac stood, taking a moment to steady himself. 'I killed her,' he said softly.

Seyeh's brow furrowed as she straightened. 'Mistress Canyon?' she asked doubtfully.

He shook his head, gazing into space. 'Neesh,' he replied. 'It be me returning with her that night and me who gave her the handkerchief after I be finding it in the rushes.'

Seyeh opened her mouth to reply, but he turned and began to walk to the track, his pace quickening. She followed, Oscar standing for a moment and then setting off after them, carrying his own guilt after revealing to Hale Owens that he'd seen Isaac sneaking in and out of the men's dormitory on a number of occasions.

They reached the track branching off to the east and took the turn, Seyeh struggling to keep up, holding up the hem of her dress as she waddled and Oscar walked beside her. Isaac's haste increased the distance between them, the need to see Oneesha causing his aches to be temporarily forgotten.

He rushed through the entrance of the long meadow and made his way towards the willow, seeing other slaves already gathered amidst the grasses before the tree. He slowed as he drew closer, the reality of what he was about to see causing his steps to falter.

'May the Lord bless you and keep you,' prayed Cesar as he stood at the head of the small group and Isaac drew alongside, his gaze falling on the dreadful sight within the branches.

'May His grace shine upon you and your sins be forgiven so that you may take your place by his side, there to dwell in liberty forevermore. Amen,' he finished, those standing about him echoing the last word and raising their heads.

Isaac moved forward, silent tears rolling down his cheeks as he stared at Oneesha's face, her right cheek and eye swollen.

'Hold your horses, nigger,' stated Pete, moving to block Isaac's passage and adjusting his grip on the rifle in his hands.

He slowly turned his gaze to the farmhand. 'I be taking her down,' he stated hoarsely.

Pete shook his head. 'No you ain't.'

Isaac looked at him with desolate bewilderment.

'Mr Canyon ain't having those who murdered his family buried on these here grounds.'

'Then I be taking her away from here and bury her in the woods,' said Isaac.

'They're both staying where they hang,' stated the farmhand firmly, raising the barrel of his rifle. 'Now step back or it'll be time in the hole for you.'

'You be doing her wrong.'

'I said, step back,' repeated Pete.

Isaac took a step forward and the barrel was put to his stomach. He stared at the farmhand, gaze challenging him to pull the trigger.

Breathless and sweating profusely, Seyeh hurried to his side and took hold of his arm. 'Isaac,' she said softly, trying to draw him away.

He turned to her, the look in his eyes causing gooseflesh to rise upon her arms. 'She be no killer and deserve better than this,' he said, eyes glistening and body beginning to tremble.

Oscar walked up and took his other arm. 'There be nothing to be done unless you want time in the hole or a bullet,' he stated, he and Seyeh beginning to lead him away from the tree.

Isaac allowed himself to be led, head bowing as he began to cry. His mouth stretched wide as the tears fell, throat and chest so constricted by his grief that no sound issued forth.

He stumbled as his legs gave way beneath him, Seyeh and Oscar losing their grasp and Isaac falling to his knees. His sorrow finally found voice and a terrific cry of agony arose from the depths of his being.

All heads turned to the sound, Seyeh beginning to weep once more as she witnessed his desolation. He clasped his knees, the tautness of his stomach drawing him in upon himself as he shook his head and longed for oblivion.

30

Isaac stirred in the stillness, his eyes opening to find there was a total absence of light, the interior of the cabin stolen away in the deep folds of the night.

He listened intently. The silence had a presence and woven into its pressing ache had been a voice which was more felt than heard.

'Neesh?' he asked the darkness as he sat up slowly.

His gaze moved to where he knew Anthony's cot rested in the pitch, its emptiness apparent despite the lack of illumination.

The whisper pressed against his eardrums once again.

He slipped from beneath the cover, feet barely making a sound as they settled on the floorboards. Pausing a moment to gather his strength, he stood on legs weakened by the events of the previous days.

Trusting his familiarity with the interior, he carefully padded to where he knew the door to be, holding his hands before him as he approached its location. His fingers came into contact with the wood and he sought out the handle, taking hold and stepping out into the night.

Isaac glanced around, able to see only a little more than he had in the dormitory. He glanced to the heavens, seeing a multitude of stars scattered like seed across the darkness. His sight settled on the new moon, which hung in the sky wearing a veil of shadow as if in mourning.

He stared at its darkened form for a few moments, savouring the slight breeze that brushed his cheeks with cool fingers.

The whisper came upon him once again and Isaac shivered involuntarily as he lowered his gaze. 'Neesh,' he said, turning and walking to the track.

He passed east when he reached the fork, steps steady and measured. His heart was drawing out before him, reaching ahead to the figure of his love. He could feel her waiting, hear her calling.

Isaac entered the meadow, a trace of mist hanging low over the river, tendrils reaching through the rushes to caress the field's edge. He walked on, the willow but a patch of deep darkness looming before him.

Moving beneath the boughs, he came to a stop, keeping his sight averted from the two bodies hanging before him. He spied a touch of paleness against the ground and narrowed his eyes, seeing the posy laying mangled in the dust.

'Never to bear fruit,' he commented, the thought coming to mind as a feeling of melancholy arose within.

He knew what he must do and stepped to the trunk. With great effort, Isaac hauled himself up into the crook where it divided. He climbed to the right and crawled along the branch upon which he'd sat when waiting for Oneesha less than a week before, passing over Anthony's beaten and bedraggled form to where she hung in silence.

Struggling to undo the rope, he finally loosed the knot and braced himself. Pulling it free, Oneesha's body dropped and he winced as it thumped against the earth, crumpling into a sorry heap.

Leaping down, he fell upon his knees and gathered her into his arms. He rocked gently on his heels, eyes closed to the horrifying sight of her dirtied and swollen face. The murmuring of the waters drifted to him in his misery. He heard the rivers voice and lifted his head.

Turning, Isaac looked out across the meadow, listening to the whisper. He rose to his feet with Oneesha draped against his chest, her arm trailing over the side like a withered branch.

He walked dreamily from beneath the boughs of the willow, passing into the bowed grasses. The words of the song she'd sung to him drifted into his mind as he carried her to the river and he began to sing with mournful softness.

'Willow, sweet willow, cry no tears for me, I'll be gone by sun-up, this rope will set me free. Willow, sweet willow, bow your head no more, the river banks are swollen, with tears I shed before.

'Mine has been a troubled life, they've hung me here to dry, the shackles no longer chain me down, there's no need to cry.

'Willow, sweet willow, cry no tears for me, I'll be gone by sun-up, this rope will set me free. Willow, sweet willow, bow your head no more, the river banks are swollen, with tears I shed before.

'This I say with my last breath, the Lord he waits for me, by His side I'll be no slave, so cry no tears for me.

'Willow, sweet willow, cry no tears for me, I'll be free by sun-up, this rope is liberty. Willow, sweet willow, bow your head no more, the river calls me onward, to a distant shore.'

Tears steaming down his cheeks, Isaac came to a stop and stood upon the bank. He looked down at Oneesha and smiled sadly.

'We be together soon,' he said, stroking her cheek before stepping into the swollen waters.

The irresistible pull of the current dragged his legs from beneath him and rolled him under the surface. Isaac didn't struggle, but retained his hold on Oneesha, hugging her close as the pressure in his lungs slowly built.

Releasing his last breath when the strain became unbearable, he felt the water filling his mouth and rushing down his throat. Fire erupted in his lungs and his thoughts began to fade. His arms lost their strength, Oneesha's body drifting loose.

And in his drowning eyes he saw her. She was smiling in the darkened depths before him, her eyes sparkling like the heavens. She beckoned for him to follow as she was drawn away by the current, calling him to the freedom that awaited.

If you enjoyed *The Hanging Tree*, then try one of the author's acclaimed historical novels set in the far south-west of England. Entitled *Where Seagulls Fly*, *Song of the Sea* and *The Shepherd of St Just*, all are set in the Middle Ages and tell the evocative stories of social outcasts. They are available as paperbacks and Kindle editions.

Look out for Edwin Page's second book set in the time of slavery. Called *Runaway*, it is a tale of innocence, acceptance and freedom. It tells the story of Joshua, a runaway slave who finds refuge on a farmstead in Missouri in 1863. Due for release on 27th May 2016, it will be available in Kindle and paperback formats.

Printed in Great Britain
by Amazon